STEVE JOBS

AMERICAN GENIUS

STEVE JOBS

AMERICAN GENIUS

by AMANDA ZILLER

◯ Collins

An Imprint of HarperCollinsPublishers

Collins is an imprint of HarperCollins Publishers.

Copyright © 2011 by HarperCollins
All rights reserved. Printed in the United States of America.
No part of this book may be used or reproduced in any manner whatsoever
without written permission except in the case of brief quotations embodied
in critical articles and reviews. For information address HarperCollins
Children's Books, a division of HarperCollins Publishers,
10 East 53rd Street, New York, NY 10022.
www.harpercollinschildrens.com

Library of Congress Cataloging-in-Publication Data is available.
ISBN 978-0-06-219765-8 (trade bdg.)

11 12 13 14 15 LP/BR 10 9 8 7 6 5 4 3 2 1
❖
First Edition

For Dad, Mom, GG, GJ, Maggie, and Max

Contents

STEVE
JOBS

AMERICAN GENIUS

Only Connect

Do you have an iPod, an iPhone, or an iPad? Have you ever downloaded a song from iTunes? Do you have a favorite app?

Our personal computers, laptops, MP3 music players, and smartphones have become such a huge part of our lives that it's hard to imagine what the world would be like without them. Until only about thirty years ago, these products did not even exist.

When Steve Jobs was twenty-one years old, he started a company with his best friend, Steve Wozniak. They decided to call it Apple Computer, and a few years after they began building computers in Jobs's garage, Apple had grown into a billion-dollar business. John Sculley, who was CEO of Apple from 1983 to 1993, said this about Apple cofounder Steve Jobs: "[Jobs] believed that the computer was eventually going to become a consumer product. That was an outrageous idea back in the early 1980's." Many of Jobs's ideas may have seemed outrageous to others of his time, but without his innovations, the way we live would be very different today.

If it weren't for Steve Jobs, we wouldn't have:

- Computers with a screen monitor, keyboard, and mouse
- Computer screens that can display icons, pictures, videos, etc.
- A mouse that can move in all directions, drag and drop, and double click
- A huge choice of fonts, or fonts named after famous cities around the world (Chicago, Geneva, London, New York, and Venice are just a few examples)
- Pixar movies and characters such as Woody, Buzz Lightyear, Nemo, WALL•E, and Lotso
- The iPod and iTunes
- The iPhone, the App Store, and electronic devices with motion sensors (the technology that makes the screen on the iPhone flip when you turn it sideways)
- The iPad and the iBookstore

Steve Jobs's impact on our world has been enormous. He has often been compared to many of the world's greatest inventors: Thomas Edison, Henry Ford, Alexander Graham Bell, and others. Like Edison, Jobs brought great changes to the world through technological advancements. Jobs personally admired and modeled his career after Edwin H. Land, the inventor of instant photography and cofounder of the Polaroid Corporation. According to Jobs, what he and Land had most in common was that they both "saw the intersection of art and science and business."

"Technology alone is not enough," Jobs said. "It's technology married with liberal arts, married with the humanities, that yields us the result that makes our heart sing." Jobs also believed, "It isn't the consumers' job to know what they want." These two tenets greatly influenced his approach to the world around him. Maybe because he was interested in so many different things, he was able to imagine how the development of new technologies could help people. From an early age, he was immersed in electronic engineering. He had a deep understanding of the science behind building electronic devices. But he also had the artistic creativity to adapt science to fit people's needs—often before the world even knew what it needed.

1 Origins

When asked about his origins, Steve Jobs said, "I was born in San Francisco, California, USA, planet Earth, February 24, 1955." He was adopted at birth by Paul and Clara Jobs. His biological mother, Joanne Schieble (who eventually took the name Joanne Simpson), later worked as a speech therapist. His father, Abdulfattah "John" Jandali, was a Syrian who became a political science professor. They met at the University of Wisconsin, where they were both graduate students.

Jobs was always known to be quite private about his personal life, but in the years before his death, he opened up to his biographer, Walter Isaacson. Joanne Schieble grew up in rural Wisconsin. Her parents were German and very religious Catholics. Jandali was from a wealthy and influential Syrian family. He described Joanne's father as "a tyrant," and, according to Isaacson, her father threatened to disown Joanne if she married an Arab. For this reason, as well as because they were only twenty-three years old at the time and both still in graduate school, they chose to give their son up for adoption.

Jobs's father has since told reporters that Schieble "upped and left [Wisconsin, where they were living at the time] to move to San Francisco to have the baby without anyone knowing, including me." Jandali claims that he would have chosen to keep his son if it had been solely up to him but that he wanted to support Schieble's wishes at the time.

Schieble told her doctor she felt very strongly that her child's adoptive parents should be highly educated. Originally, a lawyer and his wife were planning to adopt her son. However, when the baby was born, they decided that they wanted a girl and backed out of the adoption. The next couple on the list were Paul and Clara Jobs. Paul Jobs was a working-class machinist who had not finished high school, and Clara Jobs had not completed her college education.

At his 2005 Stanford University commencement address, Steve Jobs shared some of his personal story with the graduating class. He told them that when his biological mother learned that his adoptive parents were not college graduates, she "refused to sign the final adoption papers. She only relented a few months later when my parents promised that I would someday go to college." According to the authorized biography, *Steve Jobs*, by Walter Isaacson, Paul and Clara Jobs signed a pledge to start a savings account for their son's college education. Even if she didn't feel ready to raise a child herself, it's clear by his biological mother's actions that she cared deeply for his well-being.

A few months after Jobs's birth and adoption, his birth parents married. Joanne Schieble's father passed away around this time, and maybe she felt free to make her own decisions. Jandali has recently said, "I think after we got back together, Joanne had second thoughts about adoption, but by then, there was nothing we could do about it. If we had just held off for a few months, then we would have been able to raise Steve as our own, but sadly, that was not the case. We often spoke of our son and how we both wished he was with us."

Two years after they had Steve and married, Schieble and Jandali had another child, a daughter named Mona. They raised her until she was four years old. The couple divorced, and Jandali became an absentee father to Mona. He did not have a relationship with her until years later. Because Jobs's adoption was a closed adoption, Steve had no contact with his birth parents as a child. It was only as an adult that he discovered he had a biological sister.

Imagine how Jobs's life could have turned out differently if he had been kept by his birth parents, adopted by the lawyer and his wife, or maybe adopted by another couple if his birth mother had never agreed to sign the adoption papers for Paul and Clara Jobs.

Jobs's early childhood experiences shaped his mind and his personality, making him the man he would become. His parents were always open with him about discussing his adoption, focusing on the fact that they chose him and that he was special. Maybe it gave him a sense of his own uniqueness and the courage to be a truly independent thinker. Even though he was adopted, Jobs said in his biography that Paul and Clara were "my parents 1000%."

Steve Jobs described his father, Paul, as "a genius with his hands." A high school dropout, Paul joined the coast guard in World War II. Jobs told his biographer a story about how his parents met and married. Paul's friends bet him that he couldn't find a woman to marry in a two-week time frame. He won the bet and Clara as his bride.

Paul worked for many different technology companies throughout the years. Steve Jobs remembered his father teaching him how to build things from a very early age. "He had a workbench out in his garage where, when I was about five or six, he sectioned off a little piece of it and said 'Steve, this is your workbench now.' And he gave me some of his smaller tools and showed me how to use a hammer and saw and how to build things. It really was very good for me. He spent a lot of time with me . . . teaching me how to build things, how to take things apart, put things back together." Jobs's mother, Clara, held a variety of different jobs, including working as an accountant, a schoolteacher, and a bookkeeper. She taught her son how to read when he was only three years old.

Jobs said that his parents were always supportive of him. World War II veteran Gene Tankersley lived across the street from the Jobs family. He has said, "Paul was very good about helping the kids with whatever they wanted to do."

Besides working side by side with his son at their garage workbench, Paul Jobs would often take him along on weekend visits to junkyards. In a 1997 interview with *New York Times* reporter Steve Lohr, Steve Jobs described how his father would buy junkyard cars for fifty dollars, fix them up, and sell them for huge profits. He said, "That was my college fund."

When Steve was two years old, Paul and Clara adopted a daughter, Patty. Three years later, in 1960, Paul's company transferred him to its office in Palo Alto, and the family moved from San Francisco to Mountain View, a suburb in the heart of Silicon Valley. In his book *Infinite Loop*, author Michael S. Malone described the neighborhood as "the very embodiment of a Postwar Upward Mobile community," meaning it was an area with many job opportunities.

The Most Wonderful Place to Grow Up

2

In many ways, Steve Jobs's education began long before he started attending school.

Jobs had always worked with his father at his workbench in the garage, but in Mountain View, he was also surrounded by a neighborhood full of engineers. This environment was optimal for exposing the young Jobs to electronics.

Silicon Valley was naturally beautiful. Jobs described his childhood home as mainly "orchards—apricot orchards and prune orchards—and it was really paradise. I remember the air being crystal clear, where you could see from one end of the valley to the other." Beyond its physical beauty, Silicon Valley was also a hotbed for budding high-tech companies.

The area had a rich history of being the home of new technologies since the turn of the century. Charles Herrold started a school for radio engineers in 1909, and the firm that would become the Federal Telegraph Company was founded in the same year. Edwin Pridham and Peter L. Jensen invented the moving-coil loudspeaker and sold it out of a garage in Napa in 1917. In 1930, Philo T. Farnsworth of San Francisco won the television patent, and in 1932 an engineer named Charles Litton Sr. changed the way vacuum tubes were manufactured. The invention of the klystron tube by brothers Russell and Sigurd Varian, in 1939, gave the United States and the Allied powers superior radar technology over the enemy during World War II.

In the years just preceding Steve Jobs's birth, however, technology in the region *really* began to take off. In 1939, David Packard and William Hewlett had begun working out of a garage in Palo Alto, where they started their company, Hewlett-Packard. They were encouraged by their mentor, Frederick Terman, who had been their professor at Stanford. According to a historical account on Stanford University's website, "That garage would later be dubbed 'the Birthplace of Silicon Valley.'" (The term *Silicon Valley* was coined in 1971 when the journalist Don Hoefler used it as the title for a series of articles about the electronics industry.) By the time Jobs started elementary school, Hewlett-Packard was known as one of the best and most creative technology companies. Every engineer wanted to work there, and the community was filled with brilliant minds.

In 1951, only four years before Jobs was born, Professor Frederick Terman helped found what would come to be known as Stanford Research Park. This was a huge research facility in Silicon Valley that would provide space for private technology companies. In return, the companies would work closely with Stanford students to help develop their ideas for the real business world. By coincidence, one of the first companies to occupy Stanford Research Park was Varian Associates, a technology company where Clara Jobs had a position as a bookkeeper.

The development of semiconductors was a turning point in the history of Silicon Valley, especially for Steve Jobs. A semiconductor is a material that can conduct electricity and is the building block for all modern electronics. Radios, computers, telephones, and many other devices all use semiconductors. Different materials can be used to make semiconductors, but the most common material used in commercial electronics is silicon. In 1955 and 1956, William

Shockley started a company that built semiconductors, the precursors to microprocessor chips.

From that point on, the use of semiconductors was refined by engineers who formed a variety of start-up companies. This culture paved the way for Steve Jobs and Steve Wozniak to start their own company later. In 1957, Robert Noyce and Gordon Moore, leading a group of engineers nicknamed "the Traitorous Eight," left Shockley to form Fairchild Semiconductor. In 1968, they cofounded Intel. Intel is now the world's largest maker of semiconductor chips, and its microprocessors are now the standard computer chips in most personal computers.

Silicon Valley entrepreneur Steve Blank gives credit to Fairchild Semiconductor for scientific advances *and* for changing the experimental culture of Silicon Valley:

> *"The history of Fairchild was one of applied experimentation. It wasn't pure research, but rather a culture of taking sufficient risks to get to market. It was learning, discovery, iteration and execution. The goal was commercial products, but as scientists and engineers the company's founders realized that at times the cost of experimentation was failure. And just as they don't*

punish failure in a research lab, they didn't fire scientists whose experiments didn't work. Instead the company built a culture where when you hit a wall, you backed up and tried a different path. . . . The Fairchild approach would shape Silicon Valley's entrepreneurial ethos: In start-ups, failure was treated as experience."

Surrounded by so much creative energy, it's no wonder that, as a boy, Steve Jobs was excited about becoming involved in these industries. He said himself, "It was really the most wonderful place in the world to grow up" and described how the history of Silicon Valley affected him personally. "There was a man who moved in down the street, maybe about six or seven houses down the block, who was new in the neighborhood with his wife, and it turned out that he was an engineer at Hewlett-Packard and a ham radio operator and really into electronics. What he did to get to know the kids on the block was rather a strange thing: He put out a carbon microphone and a battery and a speaker on his driveway where you could talk into the microphone and your voice would be amplified by the speaker." This neighbor, Larry Lang, ended up teaching Steve Jobs a lot about electronics.

Jobs's father was his first mentor in the field of mechanics and building things, but he had his limitations. One time Jobs remembered in particular was when he told his father about Larry Lang's battery-operated speaker. "I was always taught that you needed an amplifier to amplify the voice in a microphone for it to come out in a speaker. My father taught me that. I proudly went home to my father and announced that he was all wrong and that this man up the block was amplifying voice with just a battery. My father told me that I didn't know what I was talking about and we got into a very large argument. So I dragged him down and showed him this."

Lang and Jobs built Heathkits together. The Heath Company sold kits that included instructions and all the parts needed to build things such as radios, amplifiers, phonographs, and other electronic products. Jobs recalled his experience building with Lang:

> "These Heathkits would come with these detailed manuals about how to put this thing together and all the parts would be laid out in a certain way and color coded. You'd actually build this thing yourself. I would say that this gave one several things. It gave one an understanding of what

was inside a finished product and how it worked because it would include a theory of operation. But maybe even more importantly it gave one the sense that one could build the things that one saw around oneself in the universe. These things were not mysteries anymore. I mean you looked at a television set you would think that 'I haven't built one of those but I could. There's one of those in the Heathkit catalog and I've built two other Heathkits so I could build that.' Things became much more clear that they were the results of human creation, not these magical things that just appeared in one's environment, that one had no knowledge of their interiors. It gave a tremendous level of self-confidence, that through exploration and learning one could understand seemingly very complex things in one's environment. My childhood was very fortunate in that way."

Just as its fruit orchards thrived in the rich soil of Silicon Valley, it seems that the culture and creativity of the area were ideal for providing bright, young Steve Jobs with the necessary experiences that would allow him to flourish later in life.

3 An Elementary Troublemaker

Steve Jobs showed signs of being remarkable from an early age. By the time he was five, he was building machines with his dad in the garage. Ironically, the extremely intelligent Steve Jobs did not always feel at home in the classroom. His years at Monta Loma Elementary School in Mountain View, California, were not always easy.

Jobs once said, "School was pretty hard for me at the beginning." He already knew how to read. He was already building radios with his neighbor, Larry Lang, and helping his dad build cars on the weekends. "I wanted to read books because I loved reading books and I wanted to go outside and chase butterflies," Jobs said of his early elementary years. "You know, do the things that five year olds like to do."

Jobs had a wide array of interests: science and math, books and reading. He also wasn't the first of history's geniuses to struggle in school. The scientist Albert Einstein, the political leader Winston Churchill, and the author and playwright George Bernard Shaw, all Nobel Prize winners, had a difficult time in school.

It's likely that since Jobs was so intelligent, he wasn't challenged enough by his teachers. Unfortunately, his boredom often resulted in his causing trouble. Jobs has said, "By the time I was in third grade, I had a good buddy of mine, Rick Farentino, and the only way we had fun was to create mischief. I remember we traded everybody. There was a big bike rack where everybody put their bikes, maybe a hundred bikes in this rack, and we traded everybody our lock combinations for theirs on an individual basis and then went out one day and put everybody's lock on everybody else's bike and it took them until about ten o'clock that night to get all the bikes sorted out. We set off explosives in teachers' desks. We got kicked out of school a lot."

Eventually, however, Jobs was able to find his niche when he was finally matched with the right teacher. Mrs. Hill taught fourth grade at Monta

Loma Elementary, and Jobs has called her "one of the other saints of my life."

In a strange twist of fate, his troublemaking led to Jobs's being placed in Mrs. Hill's class. "They were going to put Rick Farentino and I into the same fourth grade class, and the principal said at the last minute 'No, bad idea. Separate them.' So this teacher, Mrs. Hill, said 'I'll take one of them.'"

One of the ways that Mrs. Hill found to motivate Jobs was through bribery. "She watched me for about two weeks and then approached me. She said, Steven, I'll tell you what. I'll make you a deal. I have this math workbook and if you take it home and finish on your own without any help and you bring it back to me, if you get it 80% right, I will give you five dollars and one of these really big suckers she bought and she held it out in front of me. One of these giant things. And I looked at her like 'Are you crazy lady'? Nobody's ever done this before and of course I did it. She basically bribed me back into learning with candy and money."

Bribery might not be the best way to motivate every student, but it seemed to work well for Jobs. It was a way to interest him in schoolwork again and to change the negative feelings he already had toward school. According to Jobs, "What was really remarkable was before very long I had such a respect for her that it sort of re-ignited my desire to learn. She got me kits for making cameras. I ground my own lens and made a camera. It was really quite wonderful. I think I probably learned more academically in that one year than I learned in my life."

After excelling in his fourth-grade classroom, Jobs was tested to see whether he should skip to a higher grade level. It wasn't uncommon at that time for advanced students to skip a grade. In Jobs's case, the school wanted him to skip two grades. "My parents said 'No,'" Jobs said, adding, "Thank God." He was grateful to them for making the decision to allow him to "skip one grade but that's all."

In fact, just skipping one grade was difficult enough for Jobs. He said it was "troublesome in many ways. . . . It did create some problems." Skipping a grade can be hard socially because of the age gap it creates with classmates. For Jobs, it was even rougher. Skipping to sixth grade meant leaving elementary school altogether to attend Crittenden Middle School. Crittenden was known for being a rough school, where kids might carry knives or have fights in the bathroom. Being a year younger made Jobs an easy target for bullying.

Jobs made it through sixth grade, but halfway

through seventh grade he had a serious discussion with his parents. He told them about what went on at the school and said that he wouldn't go there one more day. He begged them to put him in another, better school. Paul Jobs recalled his son's resolution: "He said he just wouldn't go. So we moved." In 1967, the Jobs family moved to Sunnyvale, California. The section of Sunnyvale where they lived was one of the first neighborhoods to become part of Silicon Valley. The school Jobs attended, Cupertino Junior High School, was in one of the best public school districts in the area. The move to Sunnyvale would change the course of Jobs's life in many key ways.

4 A First Job for Jobs

Even after moving to Sunnyvale, Jobs still kept in close contact with his former neighbor, Larry Lang. Jobs would visit Lang's house and spend time in his garage, assembling Heathkits. Lang also introduced Jobs to the Hewlett-Packard Explorers Club.

Once a week, the club would meet at Hewlett-Packard, and an engineer from the company would give a lecture about the latest projects the company was developing. In *Steve Jobs*, Jobs tells Walter Isaacson, "I saw my first desktop computer [at Hewlett-Packard]. It was called the 9100A, and it was a glorified calculator but also really the first desktop computer. It was huge, maybe forty pounds, but it was a beauty of a thing. I fell in love with it."

Through the Explorers Club, Jobs was encouraged to work on independent projects. Jobs decided he would build a frequency counter. A frequency counter is a machine that measures the number of electronic pulses per second in an electronic signal. Some of the parts he needed were manufactured by Hewlett-Packard. "Back then, people didn't have unlisted numbers," Jobs said. He looked up William Hewlett's name in the phone book. The official story, as posted on Hewlett-Packard's website, goes like this: "Jobs called and asked, 'Is this the Bill Hewlett of Hewlett-Packard?' 'Yes,' said Bill. Jobs made his request. Bill spent some time talking to him about his project. Several days later, Jobs went to HP and picked up a bag full of parts that Bill had put together for him."

Not only did Bill Hewlett offer Jobs the parts he needed, but Jobs also received an offer to work. The summer after his freshman year at Homestead High School, Jobs worked alongside Hewlett-Packard employees on an assembly line in a plant that manufactured the kind of frequency counter he had built for his Explorers Club project.

Jobs's charm and charisma have been widely reported. He was known to be able to talk to anyone and win people over. Those who worked closely with him would sometimes refer to his powers of persuasion as Jobs's "reality distortion field." This skill was clearly present from the time he was young. Of course, he was a very intelligent person, but he was also intuitive and had a great way with people. This early life experience showed Jobs the importance of reaching out to others. It also gave him the confidence to feel that if he asked for something, he might just get it. Why not take the chance? The teenager who would become one of the most influential people in history during his lifetime was already beginning to show signs of leadership and promise.

Later in his life, once Jobs was established in his success as an entrepreneur, he was known to frequently respond to emails from strangers. Notably, one ten-year-old boy named Allen Paltrow emailed Jobs at his public address. Paltrow described his intense love of all things Apple—he remembers that the message was "enthusiastic and grammatically incorrect"—as well as a photograph of the back of his head, which was shaved in the shape of the Apple logo. Paltrow was surprised when he soon received an invitation to the opening of Apple's retail store on Fifth Avenue in New York City.

Perhaps this was Jobs's way of trying to repay Bill Hewlett for his kindness. Or, maybe what Jobs learned from Hewlett was that having an open mind and taking chances on the unknown were important qualities in a business leader.

5   Go-Getter

Another opportunity Jobs had because of the town his parents moved to was to take an electronics class at Homestead High taught by John McCollum. McCollum had been teaching at Homestead High since the school had first opened in 1963. Electronics 1, 2, and 3 courses operated more like a club, bringing the most promising students together in one place.

Similar to the way Paul Jobs scoured junkyards for spare parts, McCollum scavenged around such nearby electronics companies as Hewlett-Packard, Fairchild, and Raytheon. Once, he was able to get nine thousand free transistors from Raytheon. At that time, a single transistor would have cost about sixteen dollars. They had been manufactured for NASA, but an engineer there decided they were not of high enough quality to be sent to the moon.

By the time Jobs entered McCollum's classroom, the high school teacher had collected more equipment than the nearby community college. Four years earlier, Steve Wozniak had taken McCollum's class. The smart and talented Wozniak had become a teacher's pet and been given access to McCollum's legendary and closely guarded storeroom.

Jobs had no such luck. Even though Mrs. Hill in fourth grade had helped him overcome some of his dislike of school, he was still a fiercely independent thinker. He may have considered some of the early projects McCollum assigned to be old hat and preferred to follow his own ideas.

When working on one particular project, Jobs needed a part that McCollum didn't have. Instead of asking his teacher to help him get the part, Jobs did what he'd done before. He picked up the phone and called the public relations department of a company in Detroit that manufactured the part. McCollum remembers telling the teenaged Jobs, "You cannot call them collect." Jobs replied, "I don't have the money for the phone call. They've got plenty of money."

In addition to working during the summer at Hewlett-Packard, Jobs also worked part-time at a local electronics store, Haltek Surplus Electronics, during his high school years. He learned the value of many different pieces of computer equipment. Even then, he was developing the understanding of business that would make him such a great CEO later on. His friend Steve Wozniak remembered a Saturday they spent at the San Jose Flea Market. There, Jobs found some transistors that he then sold to his boss at Haltek for a profit. Wozniak recalled, "He knew what he was doing."

6 Woz—a Kindred Spirit

When Steve Jobs was sixteen, he finally met "the first person . . . who knew more about electronics than I did." That person was Steve Wozniak. They both seemed to recognize a kindred spirit in each other.

One of Jobs's close high school friends from McCollum's class, Bill Fernandez, remembers introducing the two Steves: "Woz was next door, washing his car, and I said, 'You know, you'll probably like this guy because you're both interested in electronics.' . . . I have to tell you, there was magic in the air. I would drive up and park in the front of Jobs' family home, and there was magic. To me, it was palpable." When Jobs and Wozniak founded Apple years later, Bill Fernandez was their first technician.

Wozniak, or "Woz," had more in common with Jobs than just a shared love of electronics, even though that was what initially bonded them. They both had a sense of playfulness, as demonstrated by their mutual love of pranking. In his autobiography, *iWoz*, Wozniak said, "I never lie, even to this day. Not even a little. Unless you count playing pranks on people, which I don't. That's comedy. Entertainment doesn't count. A joke is different from a lie."

Unlike Jobs, who hated school and was raised by parents who were not college graduates, Wozniak was a good student. His father, a graduate of the California Institute of Technology, highly valued education. He worked as an engineer at a few different companies, including Lockheed. Wozniak said, "There were all kinds of interesting things lying around my house. And when you're in a house and there are resistors lying around everywhere, you ask, 'What's that? What's a resistor?' And my dad would always give me an answer, a really good answer even a seven-year-old could understand."

Wozniak was brilliant but withdrawn socially from his peers. He was known to be extremely shy. Maybe this was another aspect of his friendship with Jobs. Even though they were five years apart in age, they were at a similar level of maturity.

They also had a sense of artistry in common. "When it came down to something like building a computer," Wozniak wrote, "I remember watching all those geeks who just wanted to do the technical side, to just put some chips together so the design worked. But I wanted to put chips together like an artist, better than anyone else could and in a way that would be the absolute most usable by humans."

Both Jobs and Wozniak were really into music. They were fans of Bob Dylan and would spend days tracking down live recordings of his concerts. Maybe this is another example of Jobs's philosophy that joining technology and science with the arts and humanities is essential for true creativity and change.

Pulling pranks was a passion. Not just any pranks, though. Toilet-papering a tree or egging a house were much too boring for Jobs and Wozniak. They refined and perfected their pranks, planning and carrying them out with the same precision and artistry they'd one day apply to building and promoting the first personal computer.

Allegedly, they once painted a toilet seat gold and glued it to a flower planter at Homestead High. They hoisted a Volkswagen Beetle onto the roof of the high school cafeteria. In what Jobs called "the banner prank that sealed our friendship," they engineered a system of ropes and pulleys to dramatically lower a banner displaying a not-so-nice message as the school's graduating class walked beneath it.

Wozniak also built a small device that he could carry in his pocket. The device would mess up the television signal in a room when it was turned on. Jobs described this prank during his 2007 Macworld Expo keynote address. He couldn't get a video to work properly and told the audience of how "Woz would have it in his pocket and we'd go into a dorm at Berkeley where he was going to school, and a bunch of folks would be watching, like, *Star Trek*, and he'd screw up the TV and somebody'd go up to fix it, and just as they had their foot off the ground, he'd turn it back on. As they put their foot back on the ground, he'd screw up the TV again." Contorting his body into a strange shape, Jobs told the audience, "And within five minutes he'd have somebody like this for the rest of the *Star Trek* episode."

One day, Wozniak's mother read a story in *Esquire* that she brought to the boys' attention. Published in October 1971, the article was called "Secrets of the Little Blue Box: A Story So Incredible It May Even Make You Feel Sorry for the Phone Company." It detailed how people called "phone phreaks" had figured out how to fake the telephone companies into allowing them to place free phone calls. Have you ever noticed that when you make a phone call, you hear fast beeping noises at different pitches? Those beeps are telephone-company computers communicating with one another to connect phone calls. Now the phone companies have more advanced systems, but in 1971, it was possible to fool the computer on the other line. A blue box would imitate the exact pitch and frequency of the beeps, and the phone companies' computers would think it was another computer.

The *Esquire* article described one phone phreak in particular, a man who called himself Captain Crunch. "The makers of Cap'n Crunch breakfast cereal offered a toy-whistle prize in every box as a treat for the Cap'n Crunch set. Somehow a phone phreak discovered that the toy whistle just happened to produce a perfect 2600-cycle tone. When the man who calls himself Captain Crunch was transferred overseas to England with his Air Force unit, he would receive scores of calls from his friends and 'mute' them—make them free of charge to them—by blowing his Cap'n Crunch whistle into his end."

Since he'd first read the article, Wozniak had enlisted Jobs, and the two were on a quest to build their own blue box. The boxes described in the *Esquire* article imitated the tones of a phone-company computer. Jobs and Wozniak first attempted to build an oscillator that would produce the exact tones, then record those tones onto a cassette player. However, the tones produced by an oscillator were not always reliable. They would change slightly if the temperature was a little too hot or a little too cold. When recorded onto a cassette player, the oscillator's tones did not fool the phone company. Instead, Wozniak decided to try something new. He wanted to create a digital blue box, one that would not depend on an oscillator to produce the tones.

Captain Crunch's real name was John Draper, and Wozniak and Jobs were able to track him down and get him on the phone. Draper agreed to go to Berkeley to meet them. In the Discovery Channel documentary *The History of Hacking*, Wozniak described his excitement at the possibility of meeting Draper, saying, "I felt like, you know, like, if you were bringing the president home."

The night Draper came to visit Berkeley, Jobs and Wozniak invited him up to Wozniak's dorm room to try out the digital blue box. They called the Vatican and asked to speak with the pope. The person who answered the phone call informed them that the pope was not available. "It was, like, four in the morning," Draper recalled, laughing.

In the documentary *Silicon Valley: A 100 Year*

Renaissance, Jobs described what it meant to him and his friend Wozniak to build "the first digital blue box in the world." He said, "Experiences like that taught us the power of ideas." If they could build a blue box that could connect them with people all over the world, that was a tremendously powerful feat. Jobs said, "If we hadn't made blue boxes there would have been no Apple."

Besides giving Jobs and Wozniak both confidence in their abilities and making them feel powerful, it was their first business partnership. They worked out a system in which Jobs would provide the necessary parts, which cost about forty dollars, and Wozniak would assemble the boxes, which took him about four hours. They would sell the boxes for one hundred and fifty dollars each and split the profit.

Their early marketing campaign used a hands-on approach. They would knock on dorm-room doors at Berkeley and ask to speak with a fictional person named George. Explaining that they wanted to buy a blue box and had heard that George was building and selling them, the two friends would closely watch the student's reaction. If the student acted confused and didn't have any idea what they were talking about, they apologized for knocking on the wrong door and moved on. If the student seemed interested or showed any signs of curiosity about blue boxes, though, they would consider that person a potential customer.

As Jobs had demonstrated before, he had a sharp knack for seeing how technology could help people. He was also great at reading people. Although Wozniak built the blue boxes, he considered it just an experiment. He credits Jobs entirely for coming up with the idea of selling the blue boxes for profit.

In addition to finding customers, Jobs also paid close attention to detail when designing the boxes. Each came with a card attached to the back. The card displayed a message written in purple: "He's got the whole world in his hand." The card came with a guarantee. Any broken box brought to Wozniak with the card still attached would be fixed for free.

It's easy to see why Jobs said there would have been no Apple if he and Wozniak hadn't sold blue boxes. The experience was born out of the playful and rebellious act of phone phreaking. It allowed the two friends to earn money. And, most importantly, it cemented their dynamic as business partners.

7 Jobs Tries College

After graduating from Homestead High School in 1972, Jobs shocked his parents when he told them he was moving into a cabin in the woods for the summer with his girlfriend of three months, Chrisann Brennan.

Certain details of the house they shared showed how in tune Jobs was at that time with artistic pursuits. "Steve hung a poster of Bob Dylan over our bed," Brennan recalls. It seems to contrast with the wildly successful businessman Jobs would become. In truth, though, it makes complete sense when considering how essential it was to Jobs's philosophies on life that he stand at the intersection of science and art.

A little later that summer, Jobs, Brennan, and Wozniak were able to work together. It wasn't just a typical summer job. They would dress up as characters from *Alice in Wonderland* at a shopping mall in Santa Clara, California. It is almost oddly fitting that the two friends who would go on to invent the first personal computer and cofound Apple took turns being the Mad Hatter and the White Rabbit, two whimsical characters whose world was unpredictable and often seemingly nonsensical. Despite their huge successes, Jobs and Wozniak never lost their childlike sense of wonder and playfulness. Even nonsense could make sense sometimes, and nothing seemed impossible.

After their first happy summer spent together, Jobs left for Reed College.

Paul and Clara Jobs were determined to keep the promise they'd made to Steve's biological mother. They were dedicated to making sure Jobs went to college. Although he had been to the Berkeley campus many times while visiting Wozniak there, he didn't feel it was quite the right place for him. He wanted a school that would offer him more than just a degree, and at that time he felt that Berkeley was a "degree mill." He was also well acquainted with Stanford University but felt it was too straitlaced and serious. After visiting a friend at Reed College in Portland, Oregon, Jobs decided the small liberal arts school was the perfect fit for him.

His parents were worried about the cost, though. As Jobs said in his 2005 commencement address at Stanford University, "I naively chose a college that was almost as expensive as Stanford." Paul Jobs said, "We tried to talk him out of it," and Clara remembered her son telling them that Reed was "the only college he wanted to go to and if he couldn't go there he didn't want to go anywhere." When their son had refused to go back to Crittenden Middle School, the Jobs family had moved to another town in a better school district. When Paul Jobs had tried to stop his son from moving in with his high school sweetheart, he'd simply said good-bye and walked out the door. Paul and Clara knew that their son would not take no for an answer.

Years later, Jobs still remembered how he felt the first day he was dropped off at the Reed campus. "I didn't even want the buildings to see that my parents were there. I didn't even want parents at that time. I just wanted to be like an orphan from Kentucky who had bummed around the country hopping freight trains for years. I just wanted to find out what life was all about."

After his first semester, Jobs decided college wasn't for him. It seems strange to think that quitting college could be considered a good decision, but it was the right one for Jobs, perhaps because it made him feel freer. "The minute I dropped out," he said, "I could stop taking the required classes that didn't interest me, and begin dropping in on the ones that looked interesting."

During his first semester at Reed, Jobs had become close friends with a classmate named Daniel Kottke. After dropping out, Jobs stayed at Reed but "didn't have a dorm room." "He slept on the floor in the rooms of friends, such as Kottke." Jobs and Kottke exchanged books and ideas. Jobs became particularly interested in Buddhist literature and Zen Buddhism, a branch of the Buddhist religion that focused on achieving enlightenment through meditation and intuition. "It placed value on experience versus intellectual understanding," he said.

In order to make some extra money, Jobs said he "returned coke bottles for the 5¢ deposits to buy food with, and I would walk the 7 miles across town every Sunday night to get one good meal a week at the Hare Krishna temple." Kottke would often accompany him to the temple.

At the end of his first year, Jobs rented a place near the campus. Wozniak visited a few times and sold some blue boxes to Reed students. Jobs also made money by fixing electronic equipment used in animal behavior experiments conducted by the psychology department. One of the psychology professors at Reed remembered Jobs's high skill level with electronics. "He often didn't want to just fix something. He often ended up bringing in something that was completely redesigned."

One example of how this very free period of his life proved invaluable later on was that "Reed College at that time offered perhaps the best calligraphy instruction in the country. . . . I learned about serif and san serif typefaces, about varying the amount of space between different letter combinations, about what makes great typography great. It was beautiful, historical, artistically subtle in a way that science can't capture, and I found it fascinating.

"None of this had even a hope of any practical application in my life. But ten years later, when we were designing the first Macintosh computer, it all came back to me. And we designed it all into the Mac."

Jobs and Kottke continued to study meditation and Zen Buddhism. They also began experimenting with different diets, which Jobs felt gave him more energy. At one time, he considered himself a fruitarian, eating only fruit for long stretches of time. They had an older friend who had traveled to India after graduation. When he came back, he shared his amazing stories and inspired Jobs and Kottke. With the goal of saving up enough money to fund his own trip to India, Jobs left Oregon in early 1974 and headed home in search of employment.

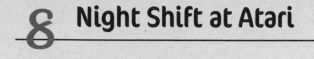

8 Night Shift at Atari

Jobs found work at a start-up video game company called Atari, now a major gaming company. When Jobs signed on in 1974, he was one of the first fifty employees to join the new company.

Atari was started and run by Nolan Bushnell. According to accounts from some of Atari's early cofounders, he ran the company with intense energy. "It was life in the fast lane with Nolan," one cofounder said. "He always wanted everything at once." It seems that Jobs may have learned about how to run a company from Bushnell by learning what *not* to do. "It was always chaos," Jobs said. "It was not a well-run company."

In an interview with PodTech.net, chief engineer Al Alcorn described meeting and hiring Jobs. The first person Jobs came into contact with when he walked into the company's offices in early 1974 was its personnel handler. Alcorn remembered her coming into his office and telling him, "We've got this kid in the lobby. He's either got something or is a crackpot."

At that time, Jobs definitely didn't seem like the type of person to work at a corporation. He looked more like a hippie. However, this was nothing new for Alcorn. Atari had a reputation among engineers as being a good company for offbeat types. The company did not have a dress code, and to Jobs, designing video games seemed more interesting than the work his friend Wozniak was doing at Hewlett-Packard.

Even though Jobs wasn't an engineer and had dropped out of college, Alcorn took a chance on him. He was hired as a technician, responsible for fixing circuit board designs.

Once he had his foot in the door, Jobs ruffled some feathers. One curious story about Jobs's early days at Atari had to do with his dietary habits. He was still experimenting with different diets, and some people found this very strange. Jobs felt that he didn't have to shower as frequently if he only ate fruit. Different people's accounts of these events vary, but it seems there were some complaints about how he smelled, and some technicians did not want to work next to him. "The engineers didn't like him," Alcorn said. "He smelled funny."

Jobs's honest but sometimes harsh critiques also offended the engineers who had more seniority than him. Bushnell and Alcorn wanted to keep Jobs, though. He was already proving himself to be a good engineer with his work on some of the early games. Bushnell has said, "I always felt to run a good company you had to have room for everybody—you could always figure out a way to make room for smart people. So, we decided to have a night shift in engineering—he was the only one in it."

When Jobs felt he had saved up enough money to travel to India, true to form, he decided to ask for something he wanted and see if he could get it. When he first asked Alcorn for the airfare to India, Alcorn said no way. Soon, though, they reached a compromise. Alcorn remembers saying, "Steve, I'll cut you a deal. I'll give you a one-way ticket to Germany—it's gotta be cheaper to get to India from Germany than it is from here—if you'll do a day or two of work over in Germany for me." Alcorn needed Jobs to help with some troubleshooting for a game that was malfunctioning. "Say hi to the guru for me," Alcorn said to Jobs as he set off for Europe.

The trip wasn't exactly fun, but it was successful. Jobs was a vegetarian but didn't know how to explain in German that he did not want to eat the meat and potatoes set before him. As for the Germans, "He wasn't dressed appropriately, he didn't behave appropriately," Alcorn said. "The Germans were horrified."

Even so, Jobs quickly fixed the problems the Germans were having with their game machines. After a few days in Germany, Jobs finally achieved his goal of traveling to India with Kottke.

9   Enlightenment

It was Jobs's dream to travel to India. But his trip was a mix of disappointment and excitement.

By arriving a few weeks before Kottke, Jobs had the opportunity to attend the Purna Kumbh festival, which takes place only once every twelve years. The religious festival involves many rituals, the highlight of which is bathing in the holy Ganges River. In *Autobiography of a Yogi*, one of the books Jobs and Kottke had shared, the author, Paramahansa Yogananda, described attending the January 1894 Kumbh Mela. Indeed, Jobs told his biographer that the only book he had downloaded onto his iPad2 was "the guide to meditation and spirituality he had first read as a teenager, then re-read in India and had read once a year ever since." It must have been an incredible experience for Jobs to participate in and witness the festival firsthand.

Neem Karoli Baba was one of the most popular gurus of the 1960s. One of his ashrams was in Kainchi, and Jobs traveled there to visit. Sadly, by the time he arrived, the guru had already passed away in September. Soon after, Kottke joined him, and the friends began traveling throughout India, usually by bus.

Jobs was as profoundly affected by his disappointments about India as by the things he found inspiring about the place. It was difficult for him to look around and see so many people living in poverty while the teachings of India's spiritual leaders had seemed to make so much sense. How could a country be spiritually enlightened while people were starving and dying all around?

Jobs remembered feeling troubled while visiting India. "We weren't going to find a place where we could go for a month to be enlightened. It was one of the first times I started thinking that maybe Thomas Edison did a lot more to improve the world than Karl Marx and Neem Karoli Baba put together."

After Jobs returned home from his seven-month stay in India, he continued his quest for spiritual enlightenment. He became very close to Kobun Chino Otogawa, an assistant at the San Francisco Zen Center who ran a visiting class in Los Altos, where his parents now lived. Jobs attended it weekly. Later, Otogawa was asked to open a full-time center in Los Altos. The two became lifelong friends. Years later, Otogawa would perform Jobs's marriage ceremony.

Another way Jobs tried to achieve personal growth was through therapy. A place called the Oregon Feeling Center offered a twelve-week course, which Jobs enrolled in. He eventually came to feel, though, that this therapy was too simplistic.

Back in Los Altos, Jobs continued meditation, and tried to get his job back at Atari.

10 Breakout

Al Alcorn remembered the day Jobs returned to his office. He presented his old boss with a book about a famous guru and confidently asked if he could come back to Atari. Alcorn said, "I put him to work again."

Jobs was given his old job as a technician. He still clashed with some of the other employees, so he stuck to his late-night schedule. During this time, Wozniak had developed an interest in video games and would often come visit Jobs when he was working late at night.

Bushnell decided he wanted to develop a single-player version of Pong. Instead of needing two players to hit the ball back and forth, there would be one player who would knock the ball into a number of "bricks" that would disappear when the ball hit them. The object of the game was to get rid of all the bricks.

The general feeling in the video game industry at that time was that paddle games were "over." Bushnell didn't believe this and still wanted to forge ahead with his plans to create the single-player game. It would be called Breakout.

Jobs was given the project, which came with a special bonus plan. In order for Atari to manufacture the game as cheaply as possible, Jobs had to use the fewest number of chips. Bushnell agreed to pay Jobs for every chip he eliminated from the design. If the total number of chips in the design was below a certain number, there was an additional bonus.

When Wozniak came to visit, Jobs told him about the project. It interested Wozniak just for the sheer challenge of the puzzle. At a book signing for his autobiography, *iWoz*, in 2006, Wozniak described the experience of making the game. He said that a "simple game like Breakout" would only take "a half an hour" to program today, using software. At the time, though, creating the game would normally have been "a six-man-month-type job."

Instead, he and Jobs did it in only four days. Four full days, that is. According to Wozniak, sleep was not an option. As Wozniak remembered it, "We went into Atari every night to work in the lab, and Steve would sit there with a wire-wrap gun, putting the wires on to wire my designs together. Something wouldn't work, I'd come over, look at something; I'd figure it out, change the circuit; he'd redo it. And four days and nights we barely got any sleep at all. We both got mononucleosis from this. And we achieved it."

In the end, they won the bonus money and the project was a great success. Breakout is considered to be a major moment in gaming history.

Apparently, the money wasn't the only thing Wozniak gained from the experience of creating the game. During the wee hours of working night after night without sleeping, he had a vision of the future. He said, "My mind was in that state when you're not awake and you're not asleep and you're thinking. Creative thoughts aren't restricted . . . you don't have inhibitions. . . . Somehow I thought about microprocessors were somehow gonna be in games someday. Yeah, you could just have programs that move the ball around!" Sure enough, this is how all games are programmed today.

Wozniak also received a job offer from Atari. In an interview for the book *Founders at Work*, Wozniak said, "Nolan Bushnell offered me a job on the spot. I said, 'No, I'm never going to leave Hewlett-Packard. . . .' Engineers—bottom of the org chart people—could come up with the ideas that would be the next hot products for the company. Everything was open to thought, discussion and innovation. So I would never leave Hewlett-Packard. I was going to be an engineer for life there."

Wozniak had no idea, then, that he and Jobs would go on to cofound what would become the most valuable technology company in the world.

11 Introducing Apple!

During his Atari job and while he and Wozniak were developing Breakout, they were also creating a personal computer.

The People's Computer Company was a local organization that distributed a newsletter and held occasional potluck dinners for computer and technology enthusiasts in the area. Its motto was "Computer power to the people." At the dinners, members discussed projects they were working on, ideas they were interested in, and the latest advances in technology and engineering. Two members, Gordon French and Fred Moore, decided to create a more formal organization, called the Homebrew Computer Club.

French and Moore's flyer read, "Are you building your own computer? Terminal? TV? Typewriter? I/O device? Or some other digital black magic box? Or are you buying time on a time-sharing service?" The flyers were left in many different places, but one posted at Hewlett-Packard caught the eye of a friend of Wozniak's.

On March 5, 1975, Wozniak attended the first meeting of the Homebrew Computer Club, along with about thirty other engineers, technicians, and computer programmers. It would later grow to hundreds of members, and its meetings every other week would be similar to science fairs, where ideas would be exchanged, designs shared, and parts bartered.

It was in that very first, small meeting where Wozniak had the idea for creating the first personal computer. The notion came to him when he was shown a specification sheet for a microprocessor.

Wozniak had already begun designing a desktop terminal and monitor that could communicate with a computer that was a distance away. When he looked at the microprocessor, he thought for the first time about the possibility of putting it inside the monitor and terminal, all in one. He said, "This whole vision of a personal computer just popped into my head. That night, I started to sketch out on paper what would later become known as the Apple I."

Microprocessors were important because they could

be capable of running a software program. At the time, there were machines called desktop computers or microcomputers. The most popular, and the one that was discussed at the first Homebrew meeting, was called the Altair. Wozniak said, "It was the first microcomputer, but it wasn't really a computer. . . . By the time you added enough RAM and everything else to have a computer that would really run a programming language, you're talking so many thousands of dollars, it was still out of the price range of anyone. It would be like $5000. . . . You needed something to run a whole computer language."

Wozniak says he became so good at optimizing because he could never afford to buy the necessary parts to build a computer. "I would design one and design it over and over and over. . . . The reason I did that was because I had no money. I could never build one."

Wozniak used his television set as a monitor. He called the Apple I "a shortcut computer." He said, "I just took the terminal that I already had." He plugged in a keyboard for typing commands. Before the Apple I, no personal or desktop computer had a keyboard and a video display. Every successful computer to come afterward did.

Now Wozniak needed to program his computer.

He had never studied computer languages at Berkeley, but a close friend sent him interesting information from his MIT courses. With a basic understanding of computer languages and programming, Wozniak set about writing his own coding language.

The Homebrew Computer Club remained an important part of the creation of the Apple I, and Jobs began going to the meetings with Wozniak to show off the computer and its features. Jobs also helped Wozniak get the parts he needed. The memory chips used in the computer were particularly expensive, but Jobs was able to convince Intel to give them some for free.

Many of the people who were interested in computers at that time did not have Wozniak's background in engineering hardware. They could program software but didn't know how to physically put the pieces of a computer together the way Wozniak did. "That's really where Steve Jobs came in saying, 'Let's start a company,'" according to Wozniak. "Steve said, 'Even if we don't get our money back, at least we'll have a company.'" Instead of selling the assembled computer, they would just sell printed circuit boards.

At first, Wozniak was hesitant. He wanted Hewlett-Packard to use his design and build his computer. When he presented the idea to the management at Hewlett-Packard, they weren't interested. They wanted to build expensive, complex computers for scientists and universities. The idea of a personal computer for everyday people and everyday home use seemed radical. Management did not see a need for a simpler, less powerful computer that was inexpensive enough for a regular person to purchase.

One night at a meeting of the Homebrew Computer Club, Paul Terrell stayed afterward to get a closer look at the Apple I. He had recently opened a computer store called the Byte Shop. He showed a lot of interest in the Apple I, gave Jobs his card, and told him to "keep in touch." Jobs, not one to waste time, walked into the shop the very next day. "I'm keeping in touch," he said.

Terrell thought the computers would sell to his customers. But he wanted Jobs to assemble the computers into a complete package. He would pay him five hundred dollars for each computer, and he wanted to purchase one hundred computers.

Wozniak prided himself on his honesty, even when Jobs had just made him an amazing offer. Before he would agree to sell the computers with Jobs, Wozniak checked with every single department at Hewlett-Packard, but no one was interested.

There was one small glitch. Wozniak and Jobs

needed fifteen thousand dollars to buy the parts to assemble the computers. Even after Jobs sold his Volkswagon and Wozniak sold his scientific calculator, they didn't have enough money. Jobs first approached his old manager at Haltek, the computer supply store where he'd worked as a teenager. He asked for the parts in return for a share in the Apple company. The manager did not think that it was a worthwhile business venture and told Jobs he couldn't do it.

Next, Jobs went to another computer supply store, called Cramer Electronics. He had a piece of paper that showed that Terrell had promised to purchase one hundred computers at five hundred dollars apiece and tried to convince the manager to give him the parts on credit. Jobs told him it would take thirty days to assemble the computers and deliver them to the Byte Shop. When Terrell paid for their computers, Jobs and Wozniak would have plenty of money to pay Cramer Electronics back for the parts.

The manager hesitated, but Jobs was determined to make a deal. He insisted that the manager call Terrell personally. If Terrell confirmed the order himself, the manager would agree to give Jobs the parts on credit. However, Terrell was away at a conference. Jobs would not give up. Miles away, at the conference, Terrell heard his name announced over the loudspeaker. The emergency call was from Jobs. Jobs put the manager of Cramer Electronics on the line so that Terrell could confirm the order right then and there.

Thirty days later, Jobs and Wozniak brought the fully assembled computer boards to the Byte Shop and made their first fifty thousand dollars. On April Fools' Day, their company was officially off the ground, but it still didn't have a name. When asked how they came up with the name Apple, Wozniak recalled, "I picked [Steve] up at the San Francisco airport and I was driving . . . [and] he said, 'Oh, I've got a name for the company. Apple Computer.' Both of us were sitting there trying to come up with techie names that were clever, but nothing was going to be better than Apple." Perhaps apples were on Jobs's mind because he had just been at an apple farm he helped manage in Portland, Oregon. The words "apple" and "computer" are an odd coupling. When put together, it makes you stop and think. "Apple" sounds simple and friendly. Maybe it would make "computer" sound less complex and scary.

In the end, only about one hundred and fifty Apple I computers were ever built and sold. Wozniak had used the bare-bones parts he already had in his home to build Apple I. "It was not designed to be an efficient computer from the ground up," he said. But it earned Wozniak a reputation for creating a computer design that was amazingly simple. The partners also earned money to grow Apple. Soon after their new company started making money from the sales of the Apple I, Jobs was able to buy Wozniak the parts he needed to build a new design he'd been working on. This would be the Apple II.

12 Apple Computer, Inc.

With Jobs's tenacity and business savvy and Wozniak's design skills, the friends were beginning to see a promising future in their new company.

They also had a promising new product.

Unlike the Apple I, which had been designed really as a computer board that could hook into a television and keyboard, the Apple II was the first fully designed all-in-one computer. Wozniak said, "I designed it very efficiently with very few parts— amazing design."

The Apple II also had something that no other personal computer had at the time: color. It was extremely expensive to manufacture computers with color, but Wozniak thought of a way to create color digitally—and cheaply. In fact, his U.S. patent for digital color display is still used in computers today. Once he figured out color, he began programming games as well. He said, "I had color, and then I had graphics, and then I had hi-res, and then I had paddles and sound to put games into the machine . . . there was just nothing stopping it."

Jobs realized that in addition to having a great product, they also needed a great, appealing package. He brought in a designer to streamline the computer casing. Jobs felt the power supply was another important aspect of the design. Most computers needed to have a built-in fan so that they wouldn't overheat. With his minimalist aesthetic, including a clunky fan in the overall design did not appeal to Jobs. Throughout his career, he would try to create power supplies in all Apple products that would avoid the need for a fan. He enlisted the help of an engineer he'd known at Atari, Rod Holt. Holt changed the way the power was supplied to the Apple II and eliminated the need for a fan. "Every computer now uses switching power supplies," Jobs said, "and they all rip off Rod's design."

Jobs and Wozniak knew they had an amazing product that would sell successfully. But they didn't have the money to buy the parts to make the high number of computers they anticipated selling each month. At first they decided to try selling their design to a larger computer company.

One of the biggest companies at that time was Commodore. In fact, the man who had sold them their first microprocessors, used to create the Apple I and Apple II, was an employee at the company. Jobs and Wozniak were hopeful, but Commodore turned them down.

Atari, where they had created Breakout a few years earlier, was another company they hoped might want to invest in the Apple II. Jobs called up his former boss, Al Alcorn, and asked if they could come over and show him the new computer they had built. They were especially excited to show the Apple II to Alcorn because its color screen was perfect for gaming. Alcorn was impressed, but Atari was involved in its own product launches and couldn't take on the Apple II. Jobs also asked Bushnell, Atari's founder, if he would consider investing fifty thousand dollars in return for one-third of the company. "I was so smart, I said no," Bushnell has said in recent years. "It's kind of fun to think about that, when I'm not crying."

Bushnell and Alcorn did, however, introduce the young entrepreneurs to a group of venture capitalists who eventually led them to a man named Mike Markkula. No one then was predicting that home computers would take off. Computers were still, for the most part, enormous machines that were complicated to use and only needed by scientists and universities. Many people would share one computer, purchasing time by the minute. No one except Jobs and Wozniak could imagine a world where everyone would have one computer all to themselves. When Jobs met and spoke with Markkula, he agreed with Jobs that there was a huge market for personal computers.

Markkula agreed to fund the first one thousand Apple II computers. They cost about two hundred fifty dollars to build, so this was an investment of $250,000—about one million dollars today. It was a huge amount of money, and a huge moment in the history of Apple.

Jobs, Wozniak, and Markkula became Apple, Incorporated, on January 3, 1977.

Soon afterward, Jobs and Markkula convinced Wozniak to leave Hewlett-Packard and work at Apple full-time. Wozniak was conflicted because he felt Hewlett-Packard was a great place to work as an engineer. He loved to engineer and design and he was worried about the prospect of running a company and working in management.

At first he declined, but then a friend suggested that he take the job at Apple as an engineer and not as a manager. Wozniak said, "That was all I needed to know, that 'Okay, I'll start this company and I'll just be an engineer.' To this day, I'm still on the org chart, on the bottom of the org chart—never once been anything but an engineer who works." He called Jobs that day to let him know he would quit Hewlett-Packard.

In April 1977, the Apple II was publicly introduced at the West Coast Computer Faire in San Francisco. Markkula had helped put Jobs and Wozniak in touch with public relations and advertising guru Regis McKenna. He'd agreed to take Apple on as a client and developed the now well-known logo—the apple with a bite taken out of it. Jobs used his artistic eye to perfect every detail of Apple's display. While other companies had bare tables with poster-board displays, Apple's table was covered in black velvet with a giant back-lit plexiglass version of the brand-new Apple logo.

The display wasn't the only thing that got spruced up. Markkula made sure Jobs and Wozniak both wore three-piece suits to the event. The high quality of the Apple II and the beautiful display were an effective combination. Three hundred orders were placed that very first day at the fair.

In many ways, Jobs and Wozniak were the perfect partners. Jobs was a brilliant businessman, making deals for parts, securing sales, and convincing investors to take a chance on what he felt would be the future of America. Jobs considered Wozniak a wizard of engineering and design. Perhaps most importantly, they each deeply respected the skills of the other. Wozniak said, "We added up to the total everything that was needed."

Markkula also played a huge role in the three-way partnership. Jobs said, "Mike really took me under his wing. . . . He emphasized that you should never start a company with the goal of getting rich. Your goal should be making something you believe in and making a company that will last." Markkula came up with a marketing philosophy for Apple that included three main components: empathy, focus, and impute. These three ideas were the basis for how Jobs would manage every company he ran.

Empathy meant connecting with people and knowing what they wanted and needed. For Jobs, this meant creating easy-to-use products that offered a seamless user experience. *Focus* meant that as a company, Apple needed to stay on track with regard to its main products instead of trying to pursue too many opportunities at once. *Impute* meant product design. Markkula wrote, "People *DO* judge a book by its cover," and felt that a product's outward appearance was just as important as its technical quality. This was a lesson Jobs would master over the course of his career. Every detail of the user experience would be taken into consideration, even the packaging of a product. For example, Jobs felt that someone opening up an iPod they just purchased should feel excitement, suspense, joy, and gratification.

13 The Rise of Apple, the Fall of Jobs

During Apple's early days, Markkula felt it was important to bring in another person to function as president of the company. Jobs himself admitted, "I was only twenty-two, and I knew I wasn't ready to run a real company." He still had some reservations, though. "Apple was my baby, and I didn't want to give it up." Mike Scott was brought on to the Apple team to serve as president but also to keep Jobs and his perfectionist tendencies in line. Although he and Jobs had a few minor conflicts in the beginning, they worked well together for the most part.

Jobs was extremely driven to create his own product that would be separate from the Apple II. Although Jobs had been the force behind the company's success, Wozniak was almost entirely credited for the creation of the Apple II. Wozniak continued to lead an engineering team in designing new versions of the Apple II, and the company would go on to sell six million of its various models over the next sixteen years. Regis McKenna, who handled Apple's public relations and advertising, explained Jobs's feelings well: "Woz designed a great machine, but it would be sitting in hobby shops today were it not for Steve Jobs." While Wozniak was content to continue modifying and perfecting new versions of the same computer, Jobs was, as always, more forward thinking.

In 1979, Apple had three major projects in development.

The first was called the Apple III. This computer was meant to be sold to the high-end business market. Apple wanted to compete with the computer company IBM.

The Lisa was the second computer in development. Instead of focusing on the business market, the Lisa was meant to appeal to the masses. Jobs himself led the project in the beginning and was also responsible for coming up with the name. In 1978, Jobs had a child with his longtime on-again-off-again high school girlfriend, Chrisann Brennan, and the Lisa was named after their daughter.

In the spring of 1979, an engineer named Jef

Raskin, who had joined Apple the year before, proposed an experimental project that was meant to solve some of the complexities of the Apple II. The Apple II displayed only uppercase letters and required considerable skill and familiarity with computers to operate and program. Raskin's vision was to make a computer that would be more like an appliance. He wanted to create something that the average person would find easy to use.

The most exciting aspect of Raskin's vision was the idea of having a graphical user interface (GUI, pronounced "gooey"). This technology was being developed nearby at the Palo Alto Research Center (PARC), which was owned by Xerox. Raskin urged Jobs to visit PARC and take a look at the scientists' research.

First, though, Xerox needed some convincing. Once again, Jobs used his charisma to broker a deal: Xerox would allow Jobs and a few Apple engineers to take a look at their research in return for one million dollars' worth of Apple stock. This turned out to be a good deal for Xerox. Apple was becoming such a rapidly growing company that in just one year, the stock Xerox held would be worth $17.6 million.

Arguably, what Apple got out of the deal was even better.

When Jobs went to PARC for the demonstration that day, he and the Apple engineers saw a GUI for the first time. Before this point, computers were very different from anything that we have now. The video monitor was what was called character based, meaning that it was linked directly to a keyboard. If a user typed the letter A, the letter A would appear on the screen. Commands would have to be entered manually by a user in order to let the computer know what the user wanted it to do.

The GUI at Xerox meant that the computer screen was not character based. Instead, it was what was called bitmapped. The computers that we use today are bitmapped. There are tiny pixels in the screen, and the computers are programmed to know which pixels should be white, black, purple, etc. Essentially, bitmapping is how, when you look at a computer screen, you can see pictures of things instead of just characters and computer code. For an idea of what computers were like before bitmapping, think of a simple calculator. Now think of how on a modern computer it is possible to look at photos, browse the internet, and even watch movies. All of that is possible because of bitmapping.

On the PARC computers, bitmapping made it possible to have the screen look like what the scientists there were the first to call a desktop. Instead of text characters and commands, bitmapping allowed the computer screen to display different icons that a user could open by clicking with a mouse.

Jobs headed back to the Apple offices tremendously excited. "I remember being at Xerox at 1979," Jobs said in an interview years later. "It was one of those sort of apocalyptic moments. I remember within ten minutes of seeing the GUI stuff, just knowing that every computer would work this way some day." He implemented these features in the design for the Lisa. He also discussed what he'd seen with Raskin. Raskin wanted to create a computer that anyone could use easily, and Jobs's dream was to "empower . . . people to use the computer without having to understand arcane computer commands." Raskin's project was the computer that would become the Macintosh.

Jobs, dedicated as ever to simplicity and perfecting the user experience, honed the GUI he'd seen at PARC. He and the Lisa and Macintosh teams made changes and advancements, in the end coming up with many of the features associated with all computers today. The mouse they'd seen at PARC was expensive, nearly three hundred dollars. It was very complicated to use and had three different buttons. The mouse that Apple created cost only fifteen dollars and had only one button. The Xerox mouse could move in only four directions (up, down, left, and right), but Apple's used a rolling ball and moved wherever the user wanted it to go.

Jobs and his team also created icons that would appear on the computer's desktop. The Apple mouse could drag and drop these icons by holding down the mouse's button and moving the mouse to drag, then letting go to drop. Xerox's GUI still required the user to type in commands to perform some functions, such as opening programs. Apple's, however, did not require any commands at all. To open a program, a user would just have to double click on an icon.

Another innovation that Apple developed was overlapping windows. Before an Apple engineer figured out how to design this, computers could only open one window at a time. With the new feature, a user could have many different windows open at the same time, one on top of the other. Each window had its own drop-down menus.

One feature Jobs had to fight to include was a white screen instead of a dark screen. This was more difficult to engineer and would require more power, but Jobs felt strongly that the user should have the feeling that "what you see is what you get." Jobs eventually got his way. It was a good thing in the long run, because this became even more important when people began to buy home printers and started desktop publishing. The printout would look just like what the user saw on the screen.

A major development in the computer world at this time was the release of a program called VisiCalc in 1979. It was a spreadsheet program that became vital in the business world. This opened up a huge market for personal computer companies, and it was a race between the two major companies at the time—Apple and IBM—to see who would be able to corner the market.

On May 19, 1980, Apple released its business model, the Apple III, at the National Computer Conference. It was meant to compete with IBM in the business market for personal computers. Unfortunately, it had many design glitches. As Apple had grown so quickly, the company hadn't established enough quality control protocols before shipping the computers. With the Apple II, Jobs and Wozniak had done their own tests in Jobs's garage. Now that Apple had so many employees and different divisions, this first attempt at a new design was a process that neither of the company's founders was familiar with. Thousands of Apple III computers were recalled, and the glitches were fixed, but by that time, IBM had become the major seller to most businesses.

Jobs and Apple couldn't dwell very long on this setback, though, because they were preparing for Apple to become a publicly traded company. This meant that people in the general public would be able to buy and sell small portions of Apple, called shares, in the stock market. Most companies are privately owned companies when they start out, just like Apple was. When a company becomes very successful, its owners can decide to go public.

On December 12, 1980, Apple held its initial public offering, an event where, for the first time, a company's stocks are sold to the general public. Apple's initial public offering was incredibly successful. It was the biggest since Ford's in 1956. It was also lucrative. The price of one share in Apple was twenty-two dollars on the day of its initial public offering. The next day, the price had risen to twenty-nine dollars. When they'd first incorporated the company in 1977, Jobs, Wozniak, and Markkula had estimated the value of Apple to be about five thousand dollars. By the end of December 1980, Apple was worth $1.79 billion.

Jobs himself was also beginning to get more and more media attention. He was featured on the cover of more than one magazine in the early eighties.

The following February, Wozniak was in a plane crash that caused him to have amnesia at first. His memory returned, but the experience changed his perspective. Years before, he'd taken a year off between his junior and senior years at Berkeley. He'd wanted to get a job to make some money before returning to school. That was when he'd started working at Hewlett-Packard, getting involved in the Homebrew Computer Club, and starting Apple with Jobs. He had never gone back to finish his degree and, after his near-death experience in the plane crash, decided it was now or never. Though he stayed on at Apple as an engineering consultant, he stopped working there full-time and enrolled at Berkeley. He later returned to Apple as an engineer in 1983.

Also in 1983, the Lisa computer was released, after a few scheduling delays. Like the Apple III, it did not do well in the market. Unlike the Apple III, it was a well-designed and powerful computer using cutting-edge GUI. But it was very expensive and didn't catch on with everyday people.

Apple's new product, the Macintosh, was set to do just that, though. Like Raskin's early vision, it was designed like an appliance, compact and ready to use. Its GUI was as seamless as Lisa's, but the physical design of the machine was much more simplistic. It looked like a large white box with a built-in screen and one narrow slot for a floppy disk.

As the Apple designers and Jobs were busy putting the final touches on the Macintosh, Jobs was becoming involved in a power struggle with company management. Markkula had replaced Scott as president of Apple a few years earlier, in 1981. In 1983, Jobs convinced John Sculley, then president of PepsiCo, to become president and CEO of Apple. "Do you want to spend the rest of your life selling sugared water or do you want a chance to change the world?" he asked Sculley. "It's better to be a pirate than to join the Navy." Sculley came on board.

Under Sculley's seasoned leadership, Apple was poised to make a huge splash in the world of personal computers when it released the Macintosh. A famous commercial was run during the Super Bowl in January 1984. Inspired by the book *1984*, a dystopian novel by George Orwell, the commercial showed a group of robotlike humans mindlessly watching their leader on a huge screen. A blond woman wearing a white tank top with a picture of a Macintosh computer on it runs up to the screen and throws a sledgehammer through it. At the end of the ad, these words are displayed as a voice reads them: "On January 24th, Apple Computer will introduce Macintosh.

And you'll see why 1984 won't be like '1984.'"

The Macintosh launched to great fanfare and was considered revolutionary. Jobs had by now perfected his theatrical unveilings. As the theme song from "Chariots of Fire" poured out over the speakers, the Macintosh began to introduce itself, saying, "never trust a computer you can't lift."

Jobs had taken Markkula's "impute" theory to a whole new level and earned a reputation for creating elaborate, carefully orchestrated product launches. He became an expert at creating media buzz by granting exclusive access to specific reporters he had cultivated relationships with. He would pack an auditorium with Apple fans and people in media, deliver a rousing speech extolling the virtues of a new product, all leading up to the dramatic moment that would wow the audience and garner tons of free publicity.

"The Mac made computing truly personal. It made an inaccessible process human. It was, perhaps, more like the arrival of the telephone in an era when communications happened by Morse Code tapped over telegraph lines. Or the first Kodak camera in 1888, bringing photography to the masses at a time when the art required fragile equipment and harsh chemicals."

However, it didn't sell quite as well as Jobs's sky-high predictions. There began to be some turmoil within Apple's different development teams. The Macintosh team started to feel underpaid and overworked. Other teams, such as the Apple II, didn't feel they were getting any attention within the company, even though the Apple II accounted for nearly 70% of Apple's profits.

There was another problem. In 1981, Jobs negotiated a deal with Bill Gates for his fledgling company, Microsoft, to provide graphics software exlusively for the Macintosh, one year after its 1983 release. But Apple missed its deadline and Microsoft leased its software to other companies and launched Windows, which had features that looked remarkably like Macintosh's interface. Jobs went ballistic. Decades of feuding would follow and a lawsuit that Apple lost.

To make matters worse, Jobs's longtime friend Wozniak decided after two years back at Apple to end his full-time employment for good. He had designed a universal remote control and wanted Apple to produce it, but Apple had decided not to go ahead with the project. Jobs and Wozniak were on good terms when Wozniak left, and Jobs supported him in starting his own company to make the remote controls. The media created a frenzy over the situation and tried to make it seem like the friends had had a falling out. In fact, Wozniak retained his shares in Apple and the two friends remained close through the years.

Meanwhile, Jobs was clashing more and more with president and CEO Sculley. He'd brought Sculley on and they'd worked well together for years, but Jobs couldn't share power for long. He started to feel like Sculley didn't know computers and didn't care enough about making a great product. Jobs tried to organize a coup against Sculley, and, in response, Sculley and the board of directors stripped Jobs of all his duties in May 1985. Jobs's title became "global visionary" and he nicknamed his office, in a remote Apple building, Siberia.

Jobs was distraught. His whole life was this company he had started with his best friend, and now it seemed it was all going on without him or Wozniak. The company they'd started out of his garage was now worth $2 billion and had more than four thousand employees.

In his commencement address at Stanford years later, Jobs described this moment in his life. "How can you get fired from a company you started? Well, as Apple grew we hired someone who I thought was very talented to run the company with me, and for the first year or so things went well. But then our visions of the future began to diverge and eventually we had a falling out. When we did, our Board of Directors sided with him. So at thirty I was out. And very publicly out. What had been the focus of my entire adult life was gone, and it was devastating."

It crossed his mind to try to muscle his way back in, but after everything that had happened between him and Sculley, he didn't think it was likely that they'd let him return. After spending time thinking in solitude, listening to Bob Dylan songs, and taking a trip to Europe, Jobs decided he needed to move on. As long as he could do what he loved—continue creating "insanely great" computer products—he knew he would be okay.

He decided to start his own company. Again.

On September 17, 1985, Jobs resigned from Apple and sold all but one share of his Apple stock. With this money, he started NeXT.

14 Lost and Found

In many ways, this period of Jobs's life was an exploration. He was cast out of Apple and felt completely on his own. It was a painful time and a difficult time. In some ways, though, it was liberating.

Jobs said later, "I didn't see it then, but it turned out that getting fired from Apple was the best thing that could have ever happened to me." It seems strange, but, according to Jobs, "the heaviness of being successful was replaced by the lightness of being a beginner again, less sure about everything. It freed me to enter one of the most creative periods of my life."

Maybe what happened at Apple had made Jobs reconsider his life. Maybe he felt a sense of everything being in flux and nothing being really permanent. Or, maybe, he just simply had more free time on his hands. Whatever the reason, a year after leaving Apple, Jobs began to search for his biological roots.

He learned that his mother was Joanne Schieble. With the help of a detective, Jobs discovered that Joanne Schieble had married and changed her name to Simpson and that she was living in Los Angeles.

Jobs called Joanne Simpson and arranged to meet her in Los Angeles. When they first met, she was, understandably, very emotional. She kept apologizing and told her son she'd always felt guilty about giving him up. Jobs pointed out that everything had turned out okay in the end.

His mother then told Jobs that he had a biological sister. Mona Simpson was a novelist who lived in New York. Joanne had never told Mona about Jobs. Joanne called Mona that night and told her that she had a brother but didn't tell her who he was.

Jobs flew with Joanne to New York to meet Mona. The siblings were strikingly similar in some ways. They looked alike, but they also had certain habits and preferences in common. They both loved to walk and talk. Going for a long walk had always been Jobs's favorite way to hold an important business meeting. Like Jobs, Mona was perceptive of the world around her. They were also both artistic.

Eventually, they became close and remained so.

Mona would later write a novel, A *Regular Guy*, whose main character had many traits similar to Jobs's. Mona would also deliver a deeply moving eulogy when Jobs passed away in 2011. One of the things she remembered about her brother at the time of life when she first got to know him was, "He was never embarrassed about working hard, even if the results were failures. If someone as smart as Steve wasn't ashamed to admit trying, maybe I didn't have to be."

15 The NeXT Step

Indeed, Jobs did not lose much time at all between being ousted from Apple and embarking on a new start-up. He envisioned NeXT as a company that would make hardware and software. "We basically wanted to keep doing what we were doing at Apple, to keep innovating," Jobs said. Instead of building computers for the everyday person, though, NeXT would cater to the higher-education market. Jobs wanted to build more expensive, more advanced computers. One of his first investors was Texas billionaire and future presidential candidate Ross Perot, who gave Jobs $20 million in return for 16 percent of the company's stock.

In addition to building computers, a main component of NeXT was software development, especially operating systems (often abbreviated as

OS). The OS is the computer system that allows a computer to run software applications. The most basic part of an operating system is the kernel, controlling things the computer does on its own such as reading and writing memory, prioritizing, and communicating between the monitor, keyboard, and mouse. The visible part of an operating system is what the user interacts with directly, the GUI, which is the desktop, icons, cursor, etc.

What Jobs wanted to do at NeXT was to implement two more things he'd learned from his visit to PARC back in 1979. At the time, according to Jobs, "I was so blown away with the potential of the germ of that GUI that I saw that I didn't even assimilate or even stick around to investigate fully the other two." Those things were, according to Jobs, "object oriented software and networking." Object oriented software was a way for the computer to organize and remember large chunks of programming code more efficiently than ever before. It made it much easier for software programmers to create applications. Networking meant the capability to connect to another computer through a network and was a precursor to the internet. The urge to take advantage of these technologies drove Jobs in the development of his new OS, which he called NeXTstep.

Jobs struggled to keep his momentum at NeXT. He'd already gained a reputation for being difficult to work with. He was sensitive and emotional and could be volatile, obsessive, even mean at times. But he was also known for his captivating charm and his contagious enthusiasm. His struggles with the Apple presidents stemmed from inexperience and his lack of confidence. At NeXT, Jobs had free rein, for better or worse.

In one instance, Jobs missed out on what could have been a major opportunity for NeXT. In 1987, John F. Akers, then CEO of IBM, came to Jobs looking for a new operating system for the IBM PC (personal computer). In squabbling over contract terms, Jobs lost valuable time. As IBM became increasingly frustrated, the main person at IBM who believed in the NeXTstep operating system left the company. Although IBM did pay NeXT for its operating system, IBM did not end up using it. Instead, they opted for Microsoft Windows, which had its own operating system. At that time, IBM was the largest PC manufacturer. If they had used NeXTstep, Jobs's struggling company might have had a chance to sell its operating system to many leading computer companies. Microsoft's operating system software ended up becoming the standard platform for PC.

The first NeXT computer was supposed to be released in 1987 but ended up being delayed until October 1988. It was twice as fast as Apple's latest Macintosh and a thousand dollars less expensive. Nevertheless, it was not commercially successful.

In September 1989, the NeXTstep OS was introduced. It was a fully functional, object-oriented operating system, meeting one of the goals Jobs had in mind when he started NeXT. In an interview in 1995, Jobs described NeXTstep, saying, "It is now the most popular object oriented system in the world, as objects are on the threshold of starting to move into the mainstream."

One year later, three new computers were released. The NeXTstation, at a cost of $4,995; the NeXTstation Color, at a cost of $7,995; and the NeXTcube, at $7,995. Although the NeXTcube, in particular, was a beautiful design—an eight-by-eight black cube—its sales were dismal. It is, however, on display at the Museum of Modern Art in New York City. Jobs said about his creation, "The machine was the best machine in the world. Believe it or not, they're selling on the used market, in some cases, for more than we sold them for originally. . . . We were the first people . . . and some of the only people who do that where you push a button and you request the computer to turn off. It figures out what it needs to do to shut down gracefully and then turns itself off. Of course the NeXT computer was also the first computer with built-in high quality sound, CD quality sound. It was just ahead of its time."

The NeXTcube was historically significant in at least one major way. It was the computer that Tim Berners-Lee, often called the father of the internet, used for writing the code for the World Wide Web. Berners-Lee's NeXTcube is on display at the CERN science center in Switzerland.

With all these flops, Jobs began to lose investors. In just a few years, by June 1991, Ross Perot resigned, saying his investment in NeXT was one of his biggest mistakes. By 1993, Jobs was the only investor left.

While its computers were not proving successful, NeXT was making great strides in developing and optimizing its operating systems. In 1992, Jobs announced that the newest versions of the NeXTstep OS, NeXTstep 3.0 and NeXTstep 486, would be able to run on a microprocessor simultaneously with Microsoft's operating system.

Faced with terrible computer sales but a promising future in software development, Jobs was forced to make a difficult decision. On a sad day in February 1993 that would come to be known as Black Tuesday,

Jobs laid off 280 of NeXT's already small workforce of 530 employees. He sold the hardware division of NeXT to Canon and redefined NeXT as a software-only business.

NeXT's operating system was sort of an orphan. It was remarkably well designed and ahead of its time, but essentially it had no home since no successful computer company would use it in actual computers. Time would prove Jobs correct in his prediction that "all software will be written using object oriented technology some day." Little did he know that someday anyone would be able to create apps and sell them in the App Store.

The tides started to change for NeXT and Jobs when Apple began shopping around for a new operating system for its newest models. One reporter at the time described this as "a humiliation akin to General Motors's having to buy engines from another company." Sculley had not been CEO since 1993, and the CEO in 1996, Gil Amelio, did not have any history with Jobs.

Jobs saw his opportunity and didn't let it pass him by. He called Amelio and set up a meeting. "It was the first time I had set foot on the Apple campus since I left in 1985," Jobs told a reporter at the time.

Apple had been struggling for years. While its

Apple II and Macintosh computers still sold decently, it hadn't advanced in technology. Because IBM had beaten Apple to the punch years earlier in the business market, all the software that had been developed since, such as Microsoft Windows, wasn't compatible with Apple's computers. The fact that NeXTstep's object oriented operating system made it easier for programmers to create software was appealing to Apple. In the meeting, Jobs stressed this point, making the case that people would want to buy a computer if there was a lot of software available for it.

Apple's technicians tested NeXTstep against another operating system they were considering and decided that NeXTstep was the better option. After working out a deal that gave Jobs $430 million in Apple stock, Apple purchased NeXT in December 1996. Jobs, with "a lot of experience and scar tissue," returned to Apple after eleven years.

During what was sometimes called Jobs's "second act" at Apple, he would restore the company to being not only profitable but also cutting-edge in terms of new technologies. Knowing now what Apple would become with Jobs back at the helm, it seems ironic that one industry analyst said in 1996, "It's very romantic going back to your first love, but it rarely works out."

16 "Sillywood"

Before Jobs's return to Apple, while he was in the throes of starting NeXT, he also got involved in a little business venture called Pixar.

Just one year after founding NeXT, Jobs became interested in the Graphics Group, part of the computer division at George Lucas's company, Lucasfilm. Lucas had originally developed the division to help create special effects in movies such as his first *Star Wars* trilogy. In 1986, though, he was looking to make his company a bit smaller and didn't feel the Graphics Group was quite as necessary as other parts of Lucasfilm.

In 1986, Jobs purchased the Graphics Group for $5 million. To help get it off the ground, he invested another $5 million of his own money. He served as chairman and CEO.

He was initially excited about the Graphics Group because of his interest in the GUI. An artist at heart, Jobs was attracted to anything that could eventually be used to make the user experience on a computer even better.

The Graphics Group, essentially, was a high-end computer hardware company when Jobs bought it and changed its name to Pixar. Its biggest product was called the Pixar Image Computer, which was mainly sold to a niche market of animators and graphic designers, the medical community, and the government. Forming a connection that would come to have great meaning later on, one of the early buyers of this computer was Disney. The studio was experimenting with methods of digitally streamlining the process of animation.

The Image Computer did not sell well enough to make the company profitable, though. To enhance product presentations, one employee, named John Lasseter, had created a series of short animations. These would be shown to demonstrate the computer's capabilities to prospective buyers. One of these animations, called *Luxo Jr.*, featured a small desk lamp hopping up and down on a table. In a Pixar movie, Luxo is the little lamp that hops onto the screen before the movie starts and becomes the letter *i* in *Pixar*.

When Lasseter showed *Luxo Jr.* at a huge computer-graphics industry convention, everyone was blown away. In order to make more money for the struggling company, Jobs had Lasseter run a team that would produce computer-animated commercials for outside companies such as Tropicana, Listerine, and the movie *Terminator 2: Judgment Day*.

Just as NeXT was floundering, Pixar was doing poorly as well. In the spring of 1990, Jobs decided to come up with a new strategy. He sold Pixar's hardware division and moved the company to Richmond, California. By 1991, Pixar had shrunk from an already small company of just one hundred employees to a minuscule forty-two. But just when things seemed to be going under, Jobs negotiated a deal for Disney to distribute three computer-animated feature Pixar films for $26 million. The first of these would be *Toy Story*.

We now know how well this turned out for Pixar. At that time, Pixar kept losing money as the release date for the movie was pushed back and back. No feature-length movie had ever been created using computer animation, and no one knew whether it would be a hit or a flop. Not even Jobs.

While *Toy Story* was in development, he considered selling Pixar a few different times. It was only when Disney confirmed that *Toy Story* would be released for the 1995 holiday season that Jobs decided to hang on and see what would happen.

The rest, as they say, is history. In an interview published just before *Toy Story*'s release in 1995, Jobs said, "There's a lot of hoopla about Hollywood and Silicon Valley converging. They call it 'Sillywood,' I think. Pixar is really going to be the first digital studio in the whole world. It really combines art and technology together. Again in a very wonderful way."

When *Toy Story* was released in 1995, it earned $350 million worldwide and received critical acclaim. It was one of the highest-grossing animated films of all time. Pixar was officially on the map.

One week later, Pixar held its initial public offering on November 29, 1995, when it became a publicly traded company.

Pixar has gone on to create the films *Toy Story 2*; *Monsters, Inc.*; *Finding Nemo*; *The Incredibles*; *Cars*; *Ratatouille*; *WALL•E*; *Up*; *Toy Story 3*; and *Cars 2*. *Finding Nemo*, *Up*, and *Toy Story 3* were not only among the top-grossing *animated* films of all time but were also among the fifty top-grossing films of all time. Pixar's films have also won twenty-three Academy Awards.

In 2004, Jobs worked with Disney CEO Michael Eisner to come to a new agreement for future films.

Negotiations broke down, though, and Jobs said that Pixar would actively look for other distributors. In September 2005, Eisner left Disney, and Jobs was able to successfully negotiate a deal with the new CEO, Robert Iger.

On January 24, 2006, Disney announced it would buy Pixar for $7.4 billion. The acquisition became official May 5, 2006, and made Jobs the largest shareholder in Disney and a member of its board of directors.

17 Think Different

In contrast to the huge success of Pixar, when Apple bought NeXT in 1996, NeXT was a small, $50-million-in-sales company. Amelio hired Jobs as his special adviser, Jobs making it clear that he wanted to remain CEO of Pixar and have a smaller role in Apple.

One journalist remarked in early 1997, "Apple Computer Inc., after 11 years without [Jobs], is a vastly different company, with an entirely new set of needs and goals. The question is whether Steve Jobs has become a different Steve Jobs than the one who created it."

In some ways, the Jobs who returned to Apple was very different from the Jobs who'd left. He had experienced running two companies that had years of difficult struggles before becoming successful. He had honed his management style, especially at Pixar, where for the first time in his career he deferred to others who knew more about the specific technology, in this case animation, than he did. An Apple employee who had been with the company since the eighties described the change in Jobs's manner of running meetings: "After the first three words out of your mouth, he'd interrupt you and say, 'O.K., here's how I see things.' It isn't like that anymore. He listens a lot more, and he's more relaxed, more mature."

Jobs was aware of the change himself and explained it by saying, "I trust people more." Reconnecting with his biological mother and developing a close relationship with his sister Mona had given him a wider support network. Perhaps he felt less alone in the world knowing that he had these connections.

Also, during his time away from Apple, Jobs had started a family of his own. He'd met Laurene Powell at a talk he'd given at Stanford. They exchanged phone numbers, but Jobs had to leave quickly to make it to a business meeting. He recalled, "I was in the parking lot, with the key in the car, and I thought to myself, 'If this is my last night on earth, would I rather spend it at a business meeting or with this woman?' I ran across the parking lot, asked her if she'd have dinner with me. She said yes, we walked into town and we've been together ever since." In 1991, they were married. Later that year, they had their first child, Reed, and in 1995 had another child, a daughter named Erin.

In other ways, Jobs hadn't changed a bit. A reporter chronicling Jobs's return to Apple in 1996 said, "Great products, according to Jobs, are a triumph of taste, of 'trying to expose yourself to the best things humans have done and then trying to bring those things into what you are doing.' The Macintosh, he has said, turned out so well because the people working on it were musicians, artists, poets and historians who also happened to be excellent computer scientists."

At first, Jobs was happy in his role as adviser to the CEO, Amelio. Soon, though, he began to get restless and want more power. One of the first things he did was to make sure the people that he'd brought from NeXT were placed in positions where they couldn't be easily fired and where they would have control.

Things came to a breaking point for Jobs when Amelio horribly fumbled his presentation at Macworld Expo. Numerous news stories began to surface about Apple and its demise. At the annual shareholders meeting, unable to explain why Apple's stock had gone down so far so quickly, Amelio simply lined up microphones and listened to the shareholders vent.

The board of directors was losing faith in Amelio. At the same time, Jobs was seeming like a better and better candidate to lead the company. He might have been a slightly calmer, more mature version of his old self, but he still had the same ability to be charming and charismatic. One night, Jobs got a call from one of Apple's board members asking him to take over as CEO.

Amelio resigned in July 1997, but Jobs didn't start right away. He claimed that he wanted to make sure he had enough time to run Pixar and spend time with his family. Jobs said, "We'd just taken Pixar public and I was happy being CEO there. I never knew of anyone who served as CEO of two public companies, even temporarily. . . . I didn't know what I wanted to do." Eventually, a compromise was reached: Jobs would step up his role as an adviser and act as "interim CEO" while helping Apple find a new CEO.

Jobs was the star of the Macworld Expo in Boston on August 6, 1997. After Apple had floundered for so many years, people were beginning to have faith again that it would recover under new leadership. Jobs had internalized and perfected Markkula's idea of "impute"—he knew how to inspire people. People were cheering and shouting, "Steve!" Jobs discussed why Apple had been doing badly. He said it was because there was no strategy, but that he had people who were brilliant and ready to work.

Then he had an exciting announcement. Apple had made an alliance with Microsoft. Microsoft would put out a version of Office for Mac, and Apple would make Internet Explorer the default web browser on all of its computers. After a long-standing rivalry with Bill Gates, Jobs had Gates address the audience on a giant screen. (The Microsoft chairman hadn't been able to attend in person.) "If we want Microsoft Office on the Mac, we better treat the company that put it out with a little bit of gratitude," Jobs announced to the crowd.

After Macworld Expo, Apple's stock was already beginning to increase in value, but the company still needed to create and sell some "insanely great" products.

Jobs felt he had come back home, but he was a far better leader than he would have been in years past. Early on as CEO, he made a few changes that were reminiscent of the very first version of Apple's marketing philosophy that Markkula had come up with in 1977. Jobs created focus: He eliminated more than three-quarters of the company's products in development. He removed products such as printers, scanners, and portable digital assistants from the pipeline. He wanted Apple to create only desktop and portable Macintosh computers. Although this meant he had to close plants, lay off workers, and make deals with Microsoft, it was worth it to Jobs to save the company. He also replaced most of the board, with only a few select members being allowed to stay on. Culturally, he took Apple in a slightly different direction by prohibiting employees from talking to the press unless accompanied by a public relations official.

Development and design began for a new generation of Macs, and a new marketing campaign featured such famous historic visionaries as Pablo Picasso and Albert Einstein with the slogan "Think Different."

In January 1998, Jobs happily announced to the public that Apple had its first profitable year since 1995. Jobs also announced that Apple would be opening "stores within stores" at CompUSA. There were 149 CompUSA stores in the United States, and a mini Apple store would be in every single one.

Two new computer models came out in May 1998, the iMac and the PowerBook G3. In only three months, Apple had 150,000 preorders for the iMac. It would be Apple's first new all-in-one computer since the original Macintosh. The iMac had all the latest technology, but its design was unique. Instead of having a monitor and a computer tower, as most other PCs did, the monitor and computer of the iMac were all in the same box. Apple took one risk: It did not include a floppy disk drive in the design. This turned out to be a good thing, though, because soon floppy disks became obsolete as people began to switch to CD-ROMs.

In its first five months, the iMac sold close to 800,000 units. Here, Jobs employed the third aspect of Markkula's marketing strategy: impute. The iMac was a cutting-edge machine in a beautiful package. Jonathan Ive led the design team for the iMac. Later, he would design the iPod and the iPhone.

On the heels of all these successes, Apple's stock rose to forty dollars per share, its highest price in three years. "Apple is back" stories started cropping up throughout the media. *Businessweek* wrote, "For Apple, it's back to the future. That's why the introduction of the iMac was so heavy on nostalgia. It's the machine for the rest of us—updated for the Internet Age." According to *Time* magazine, "Act III is under way . . . and, against all odds, the Apple dream is alive."

18 Insanely Great

During the past ten years, Apple has become a household name. It's hard to believe that a company that has created some of the most revolutionary products was once on the brink of going under. Through refocusing Apple on what had made it great to begin with, Jobs was able to turn everything around.

One major development for Apple in the early 2000s was to expand its retail strategy. Apple already had 149 "stores within stores" through its partnership with CompUSA, but Jobs decided that Apple should have its own store. On May 19, 2001, the first two official Apple Store locations were opened, one in Virginia and one in California.

Even in retail, Jobs had an artistic eye and a flair for beautiful design. Apple stores are not just plain brick buildings. One example is the Apple Store on

Fifth Avenue in New York City, which opened in 2006. The entrance is an enormous glass cube, with a staircase spiraling around a cylindrical elevator to the store, which is underground.

In the early spring of 2001, Jobs announced the release of Apple's new operating system. Mac OS X was an object-oriented operating system that combined the NeXTstep technology with the existing Mac operating system. The resulting Mac OS X was just as reliable and secure as it had been before but had a new, beautiful GUI. Because of NeXTstep, the operating system allowed programmers to create software in a fraction of the time it would take on an older system.

That same year, Apple made a huge innovation with its first really game-changing device since the Apple II had revolutionized the world of personal computers: the iPod.

Some people argue that what Jobs was truly great at was not necessarily inventing brand-new products out of nothing but at honing and perfecting them. By the time the iPod was released in November 2001, MP3 music files were not uncommon. With the widespread use of the internet, it had already become the norm to trade and share music online. Other MP3 players had been introduced into the market, such as

Audio Highway's Listen Up, which was the first portable MP3 player, available in 1997.

The iPod was different. Headed once again by Jonathan Ive, the team created a product that many consider a masterpiece of design. It was simple to use, with only four buttons—play, pause, fast-forward, and rewind—and one central Select button. It had a sleek, streamlined casing.

Jobs knew, as ever, how to connect the technological side with the human side. Instead of marketing the iPod the way personal computers were sold, by listing all of the capabilities of the computer's inner workings, Jobs made it simple. The first iPod had a five-gigabyte hard drive, a figure that might not mean much to the average person who doesn't know a lot about computers. Jobs said instead that the iPod could hold one thousand songs. He gave the iPod meaning to the people who would want to use it. Despite being fairly expensive at $399, the iPod was hugely popular. In its first six years, more than one hundred million iPods were sold.

The reason Jobs is remembered for revolutionizing the music industry isn't only because of creating the iPod. He was always thinking about the end-to-end user experience and trying to make technology as friendly and easy to use as possible. Many people already downloaded MP3 music files to their computers, but when this type of file sharing began, it was done for free on websites such as Napster. In 2001, the courts ruled that this practice infringed on the copyright of musicians and their record companies, and it became illegal to download free MP3 files. The problem was, there wasn't a convenient way to legally purchase MP3 music files.

Jobs recognized this problem, and also a possible solution. In 2003, Apple launched its online iTunes Store. There, MP3 music downloads were available for the relatively low price of ninety-nine cents per song. Jobs saw that people who had previously become accustomed to getting their music for free would not want to start paying a lot of money for it. The record industry at this time was in crisis. Everyone was panicking that if people shared music illegally, record companies and musicians would lose money. With iTunes, Jobs was able to meet the needs of the record companies, musicians, *and* the fans who loved their music.

It hadn't been easy for Jobs to convince the music industry to agree to his plan. Record companies had to give Apple permission to sell their music in the iTunes Store. Negotiating an agreement that worked for both parties was a task suited to a charismatic, forward-thinking person such as Jobs. Record companies mistrusted online music because it had almost put them out of business. Jobs offered them an option for downloading music online that would help the companies get their business back. Many responded with enthusiasm and signed deals with Apple to offer their music on iTunes. With his hallmark persistence, he personally persuaded artists such as U2's Bono, Bob Dylan, Madonna, and Eminem to make their music available for sale on iTunes.

After only one year in existence, the iTunes Store was a success. It had sold 85 million songs in its first year, and 70 percent of people who downloaded music from the internet were using iTunes to do so—*and* paying for their music. Within five years, iTunes was the runaway leader in online music services, with more than five billion downloads.

In addition to his dramatic unveilings of new Apple products, Jobs began to cultivate an aura of mystery around the company. For example, when he launched the new Mac OS X operating system and the iPod, he had done so from complete secrecy. Anticipation grew before any Apple event where he was scheduled to speak. Media people would attend Apple launches, bringing more attention to the company.

Even with the huge success of the iPod, Jobs still kept Apple focused on its core business: personal computers. At the 2005 Apple Worldwide Developers Conference, Jobs delivered the keynote address. There he announced that all Apple computers would begin using Intel-based microprocessors, the most advanced microprocessors of the time. Previously, Apple's use of slightly slower microprocessors had given other personal computer companies an edge in the marketplace.

As early as January 2006, the first Apple computers to use Intel were released: the new MacBook Pro laptop and the iMac. By August of that year, Jobs had led Apple toward transitioning the entire Mac line to use Intel chips, a year ahead of schedule. Apple retired the Power Mac, the iBook, and the Power-Book models, replacing them with the Mac Pro, MacBook, and MacBook Pro, all powered by Intel microprocessor chips.

When reporters had hopefully penned articles in 1998 about how "Apple is back," some may have expected to be disappointed. By 2006, it was clear that Apple was, indeed, back. In 2003, Apple's stock had been valued at six dollars per share. By 2006, it had increased in value more than ten times, to a value of eighty dollars per share.

One moment that Jobs could not resist the urge to revel in was when Apple's market value rose above that of personal computer company Dell, in January 2006. A little less than thirty years after its birth, Apple was worth $72.13 billion. Years earlier, when Apple was in crisis, Michael Dell, the CEO of Dell, had told the *New York Times* that if he were in charge of Apple, he would "shut it down and give the money back to the shareholders." When Apple's value surpassed Dell's, Jobs sent an email to all of Apple's employees that read, "Team, it turned out that Michael Dell wasn't perfect at predicting the future. Based on today's stock market close, Apple is worth more than Dell. Stocks go up and down, and things may be different tomorrow, but I thought it was worth a moment of reflection today. Steve."

At the next Macworld Expo, in 2007, Jobs announced two new products from Apple. The first was Apple TV, a product that would wirelessly connect digital media to a user's TV. It allowed people to play music, display photographs, and stream online television shows and movies on their HDTVs instead of on their computer screens or mobile devices.

The second product was the iPhone. "This is a day I've been looking forward to for two and a half years," he told the crowd. "Every once in a while a revolutionary product comes along that changes everything. In 1984, we introduced the Macintosh . . . It changed the whole computer industry. In 2001, we introduced the first iPod and . . . it changed the entire music industry. Well, today, we're introducing three revolutionary products of this class. The first one is a widescreen iPod with touch controls. The second is a revolutionary mobile phone. The third is a breakthrough Internet communications device. These are not three separate devices. This is one device. And we are calling it iPhone. Today Apple is going to reinvent the phone."

It's easy to see why so many people flocked to Apple's launch events to hear Jobs speak. His enthusiasm was palpable and contagious. After demonstrating the features of the iPhone, Jobs announced another change in Apple: the company would be changing its name from Apple Computer, Inc., to Apple Inc. This meant more than just reprinting a few business cards. In his keynote address he explained, "The Mac, iPod, Apple TV and iPhone. Only one of those is a computer. So we're changing the name."

The day after Jobs delivered his keynote address and demonstration of the iPhone, Apple's stock hit an all-time high of $97.80 per share. By May, it was over $100 per share. With strong sales of Mac computers, the iPod, iTunes, and the iPhone, Apple continued to be an innovator in the world of technology and devices.

In July 2008, the App Store was launched. Within the environment of the iTunes Store, the App Store sold applications for the iPhone and iPod touch. The genius of the idea was that Apple didn't create the apps. They could be created by companies and even individuals and sold in the App Store, with Apple receiving a percentage of the earnings. Within only one month, the App Store sold sixty million applications. Every day, it brought in an average of $1 million. One of the greatest aspects of the App Store was that it fostered two of Jobs's main ideals—creativity and entrepreneurialism—in others. It gave individuals a platform to sell applications they developed, with 70 percent of the money earned going to the developer and 30 percent to Apple.

In 1984, Jobs and Wozniak had made personal computing easy for the average user. In 2008, Apple made software applications simple to develop for the average person, too. The 70-percent/30-percent split made selling apps in the App Store attractive to people. It essentially opened up a whole new partnership, pairing Apple with anyone who wanted to create their own app. It also encouraged a huge advance in the number of applications available for Apple's iPhone and iPod touch users.

The success of Apple's products could be traced back to Jobs's genius design strategy. For Jobs, a product's design didn't mean just what the product looked like on the outside, or how it was packaged. He cared about every design aspect of a product, even the smallest details. Design was about how a product worked and what kind of experience it offered to the user. He had the vision and ability to always focus on the end result—the user experience. Combining the technological with the humanistic, Jobs figured out how a product could change a person's life.

Nine years after Apple's iPod and iTunes Store revolutionized the music industry, a new product was released that would perhaps come to influence the future of digital publishing in a similar way. On January 27, 2010, Apple announced a large-screen, tabletlike device called the iPad.

Jobs had actually had the idea to forgo a traditional computer keyboard and replace it with a touch screen in the early 2000s. An early version of a tablet personal computer that would later become the iPad was discussed within Apple, but Jobs's first thought in those days was that Apple could use the idea to create a phone. This prototype would be used to create the iPhone and iPod touch. After the widespread success of these devices, Jobs went back and took another look at the original, larger version.

The significance of tablet PCs on the publishing world was widely speculated on as rumors of Apple's development of the iPad began to circulate years before it was announced. In some ways, the publishing industry was going through a time of great change, just like the music industry had been years earlier.

To some traditionalists in the world of book publishing, ebooks seemed ominous. Publishers feared that if digital versions of books became available online, people would begin sharing the files for free, as had happened with MP3 music files at first. Authors and publishers would no longer receive payment for their work, and the book publishing industry would be in great jeopardy. Publishers also worried that ebooks would make it so easy and fast to publish a book that the roles of people such as editors, jacket designers, and marketing and publicity experts might no longer be considered vital.

In the world of newspaper and magazine publishing, there were the same concerns. These were exacerbated by the way people were already sharing so much information and news over the internet. Long-standing publications saw their print sales plummet as more and more people began reading the news online.

Some devices designed specifically for users to download and read books, newspapers, and magazines began to crop up in the market. Sony's e-reader was a very simple device that was about the size of a book. Users could transfer documents from their computers to the device and read on the go. Amazon's Kindle was more advanced, specifically designed to enhance the reader's experience, while also offering wireless internet connection so that readers could purchase and download ebooks from Amazon.com directly onto the device. Barnes & Noble followed suit with their own version of an e-reader, the Nook.

Still, none of these devices was comparable to the iPad, for a few reasons. One was that they didn't have color. The technology used in e-readers up to that point was the same technology used in an Etch A Sketch toy. Text was displayed on the screen through magnets. The good thing about this was the only time the device used power was when the user turned the page. The iPad, in contrast, would have a backlit screen, just like a computer, with a full-color display. This would make it a much better way to read magazines, for example. The iPad would also be able to connect to the internet through a Wi-Fi network, a feature some e-readers already had. However, the iPad would have the additional capability to connect to the internet via satellite, the way smartphones could; iPad users would be able to access the internet on their devices anytime, anywhere.

The largest difference between an iPad and an e-reader was even more monumental. The iPad was really the next phase of personal computing. While the e-readers were devices dedicated to only one thing, the iPad represented the future. Although the very first version of the iPad was not as fast and did not have as much memory as a personal computer or laptop, it set the stage for the next era—what Jobs called "the post-PC era"—of computers.

When the iPad went on sale on April 3, 2010, more than 300,000 were sold that very day. After one week, 500,000 had been sold, and in less than one month since its release, the iPad reached 1 million in sales. For the first time since 1989, Apple's market value surpassed Microsoft's.

As he'd done with record companies and the iTunes Store, Jobs offered publishers a place to sell their ebooks directly to Apple customers and opened the iBookstore the same day the iPad was released.

By 2010, most newspapers and magazines already had their own extensive websites where they offered online subscriptions for full access. Their sites were already accessible to iPad users through the internet, and it was a simpler transition for these kinds of publications to create apps that would optimize readers' experience on Apple devices. So many people had already begun reading newspapers and magazines on iPhones and other devices that most of these apps already existed.

For book publishers, the digital realm was more like uncharted territory. Traditionally, print books had been sold to bookstores and online bookstores at a list price that was set by the publisher. The author would receive a percentage of the list price for every book that was sold. Once the books were in the hands of the bookstores, however, the stores were free to set their own prices. With ebooks, this way of doing business became more complicated because it was harder to assess the publishers' costs of producing an ebook. Publishers worried that if people stopped buying physical books, their business would crumble. With the iBookstore, Jobs once again used his negotiating skills to work with publishers and come up with a new system. Publishers would be able to set the price of their books in the iBookstore. In this way, publishers and authors could better afford the switch to ebooks.

As of 2011, there are many devices on the market that compete with the iPhone and the iPad, most notably Google's Android phones, Samsung's Galaxy Tab, and Amazon's Kindle Fire tablets. While it remains to be seen which versions will be the most lasting, Jobs and Apple were the first to introduce large touch-screen phones and tablet computers. Jobs was also visionary in his concepts of the iTunes Store, the App Store, and the iBookstore. As the future unfolds, Apple's mark on shaping it will prove indelible.

19   Visionary

Beyond changing the landscape of the personal computer industry, the music industry, and the publishing industry, Jobs also forever changed the way people viewed corporate leaders. Jobs always operated on the principle that "there's actually very little distinction between an artist and a scientist or engineer of the highest caliber. I've never had a distinction in my mind between those two types of people. They've just been to me people who pursue different paths but basically kind of headed to the same goal which is to express something of what they perceive to be the truth around them so that others can benefit by it."

In the end, that principle affected not only the products he helped envision and develop but the way he conducted himself as a businessman and CEO.

The young Jobs had a lot to learn. He'd clashed with many of his colleagues. Maybe because he had enjoyed such early success, he didn't have as much patience for possible failure. He didn't have as much faith in other people and didn't have the close relationships he'd developed by the time he came back to Apple later in his life. After gaining experience running Pixar and NeXT, he was much better prepared to lead Apple to its current position as the most valuable technology company in the world.

One aspect of his personality that never changed throughout his life, though, was his artistic sensibility. He described it himself as "having an insight into what one sees around them. Generally putting things together in a way no one else has before and finding a way to express that to other people." According to Jobs, "in the 70's and the 80's the best people in computers would have normally been poets and writers and musicians."

A word frequently used when talking about Jobs is *visionary*. He ran his companies in a visionary way and inspired others. Jobs said one of the things that can happen when a company or even an individual stagnates is that "they settle into ways of looking at the world and become satisfied with things and the world changes and keeps evolving and new potential arises but these people who are settled in don't see it." Jobs never settled.

When asked in an interview for his advice to young entrepreneurs, Jobs said he wholeheartedly believed that "there will always be opportunity for young companies, young people to innovate." He said that there are two things that really matter to build a successful company. The first is a truly excellent product. "A lot of people come to me and say 'I want to be an entrepreneur,'" Jobs said. "And I go 'Oh that's great, what's your idea?' And they say 'I don't have one yet.' And I say 'I think you should go get a job as a busboy or something until you find something you're really passionate about.'"

Jobs said the second thing is "pure perseverance." When Jobs recognized that he wasn't getting a good education at Crittenden Middle School, he convinced his parents to move. When he decided he wanted to be at Reed, he convinced them to let him go. When Wozniak wanted to keep making computers as a hobby, Jobs convinced him they should start Apple together. When the manager of a computer supply store was reluctant to give him parts on credit, he called up the owner of the Byte Shop and had him confirm the purchase order over the phone. Even heartbroken after being ousted from Apple, Jobs continued working hard and started two companies that would go on to be successful beyond what he'd even imagined. He never once took no for an answer, and never once stopped working as hard as he could.

Along with a great product and perseverance, perhaps there is another attribute that made Jobs successful. He said, "You've got to have an idea, or a problem or a wrong that you want to right that you're passionate about." Jobs's passion was what fueled him to strive toward excellence, down to every last detail.

One story that illustrates why Jobs was such an effective business leader was posted online by Vic Gundotra, an executive at Google who worked closely with Jobs. He described one Sunday morning when he received a phone call from Jobs. Because he was attending a religious service and Jobs had called from an unlisted phone number, Gundotra hadn't picked up the call right away and had this message from Jobs: "Vic, can you call me at home? I have something urgent to discuss."

Though they had regular dealings during the week, it was unusual for Jobs to call Gundotra on the weekend, and especially unusual for him to request a call back on his home number. A bit worried, Gundotra called Jobs right away.

Jobs said, "So Vic, we have an urgent issue, one

that I need addressed right away. I've already assigned someone from my team to help you, and I hope you can fix this tomorrow. I've been looking at the Google logo on the iPhone and I'm not happy with the icon. The second O in Google doesn't have the right yellow gradient. It's just wrong and I'm going to have Greg fix it tomorrow. Is that okay with you?"

In recounting the story online Gundotra wrote, "When I think about leadership, passion and attention to detail, I think back to the call I received from Steve Jobs on a Sunday morning in January. It was a lesson I'll never forget. CEOs should care about details. Even shades of yellow. On a Sunday."

20 Live Each Day

Jobs had perfected his performances at Apple launch events and led Apple to become the most valuable technology company in the world in 2011. Most people did not know that, since 2003, Jobs had been fighting a private battle against pancreatic cancer.

In his 2005 Stanford commencement address, Jobs said, "When I was 17, I read a quote that went something like: 'If you live each day as if it was your last, someday you'll most certainly be right.' It made an impression on me, and since then . . . remembering that I'll be dead soon is the most important tool I've ever encountered to help me make the big choices in life."

At the commencement, Jobs told the graduates one of his first operations had cured him of cancer. In reality, he was still in the midst of his battle. He began taking periodic medical leaves from Apple.

Finally, on August 24, 2011, he officially resigned from Apple. In a letter sent to the board of directors, Jobs wrote, "I have always said if there ever came a day when I could no longer meet my duties and expectations as Apple's CEO, I would be the first to let you know. Unfortunately, that day has come. . . . I believe Apple's brightest and most innovative days are ahead of it. And I look forward to watching and contributing to its success in a new role. I have made some of the best friends of my life at Apple, and I thank you all for the many years of being able to work alongside you."

Although he remained chairman of Apple's board of directors and even offered his advice to executives regarding the unveiling of the latest iPhone, Jobs mainly spent the next few weeks visiting with close friends and family.

On October 5 , 2011, Steve Jobs passed away at his home in California, surrounded by his wife, Laurene, their three children, his daughter Lisa, and his two sisters, Patty and Mona.

People began sharing their stories of Jobs in online eulogies. Many went to the nearest Apple Store and left hand-drawn cards, flowers, and candles in memory of Jobs.

Both Apple and Pixar paid tribute to Jobs on their websites.

Pixar said, "Steve was an extraordinary visionary, our very dear friend, and our guiding light of the Pixar family. He saw the potential of what Pixar could be before the rest of us, and beyond what anyone ever imagined. Steve took a chance on us and believed in our crazy dream of making computer animated films; the one thing he always said was to 'make it great.' He is why Pixar turned out the way we did and his strength, integrity, and love of life has made us all better people. He will forever be part of Pixar's DNA."

On Apple's website, this was posted: "Apple has lost a visionary and creative genius, and the world has lost an amazing human being. Those of us who have been fortunate enough to know and work with Steve have lost a dear friend and an inspiring mentor. Steve leaves behind a company that only he could have built, and his spirit will forever be the foundation of Apple."

In a eulogy printed in the *New York Times*, Jobs's sister Mona said of her brother, "Steve worked at what he loved. He worked really hard. Every day. . . . He was the opposite of absent-minded. . . . He was willing to be misunderstood. . . . Steve was humble. Steve liked to keep learning. . . . Steve had a lot of fun. . . . He treasured happiness."

21 A Dent in the Universe

In Mona Simpson's eulogy, she reminded everyone, "We all—in the end—die in medias res. In the middle of a story. Of many stories."

Indeed, Jobs's work at Apple is far from finished. Before he left the company, he generated many ideas and asked people to promise to execute them. He will be missed, but his innovations and leadership continue on in the company he created and reinvented.

Pixar is the leading animation studio today, just as Jobs predicted it would be years ago, with a commitment to continuing its tradition of excellence.

Jobs was a complicated person. In the wake of his death, he was touted as a genius *and* condemned as a tyrant. It seemed to echo Jobs's own way of seeing things in black and white—as "insanely great" or completely stupid. It's impossible to separate Jobs's two sides. He was intuitive and charismatic, full of intoxicating energy. He was autocratic and overbearing. But most people would still bestow these titles on him: visionary, genius, revolutionary.

Maybe unwittingly, he summed up his own life best when he spoke at Stanford back in 2005: "Death is very likely the single best invention of Life. It is Life's change agent. It clears out the old to make way for the new. . . . Your time is limited, so don't waste it living someone else's life. Don't be trapped by dogma—which is living with the results of other people's thinking. Don't let the noise of others' opinions drown out your own inner voice. And most important, have the courage to follow your heart and intuition. They somehow already know what you truly want to become. Everything else is secondary."

Jobs spent the first part of his life developing his own connection to his intuition, through travel, through his spiritual exploration of Zen Buddhism, through therapy, and through searching for his roots. It could be said that he spent his life afterward using that intuition to create true innovations. He often rallied the employees at Apple by encouraging them to make "a dent in the universe." Jobs himself probably made more than just one.

What we can all learn from Jobs is to live life at that intersection between art and science. We need science to know how to do something. We need art to know what to do. All of us are capable of looking around us with a more open heart and mind. The universe is all around us, just waiting for us to make a dent.

Even at his last breath, Jobs viewed the world with a sense of wonderment.

His last words, shared by his sister Mona, were, "OH WOW. OH WOW. OH WOW."

Learn even more about Steve Jobs . . . by turning the page!

Milestones from Steve Jobs's Life

February 24, 1955—Happy birthday, Steve Jobs! He was adopted by Paul and Clara Jobs after being born to his biological parents, Joanne Carole Schieble and Abdulfattah Jandali.

1972—Jobs graduates from Homestead High School in Cupertino, California, and attends Reed College in Portland, Oregon, for one semester. After dropping out, he continues auditing classes.

1974—Jobs and his friend (and later Apple employee) Daniel Kottke visit India together in search of spiritual enlightenment.

1978—Jobs's daughter Lisa is born.

1985—Jobs finds his birth mother and meets his sister Mona Simpson.

1991—Jobs marries Laurene Powell on March 18.

Jobs's son, Reed, is born.

1995—Jobs's daughter Erin is born.

1998—Jobs's daughter Eve is born.

2003—Jobs is diagnosed with cancer.

2005—Jobs speaks at the Stanford University commencement.

2007—Jobs is inducted into the California Hall of Fame on December 5.

2009—In September, Jobs makes his first public appearance after his liver transplant.

2011—On October 5, Jobs loses his battle with pancreatic cancer. He dies of respiratory arrest in his California home, surrounded by his wife, children, and sisters.

A small private funeral is held on October 7, with only immediate family members in attendance.

October 16 is declared "Steve Jobs Day" by Governor Jerry Brown of California. An invitation-only memorial is held at Stanford University.

Jobs's Jobs: A Chronology of Steve Jobs's Career

1967—Jobs gets a job. Twelve-year-old Steve calls William Hewlett, then the president of Hewlett-Packard, and is offered a summer job at the company.

1971—Jobs and Steve Wozniak meet through a mutual friend.

1974–1976—Jobs works as a technician for the gaming company Atari.

1975—Jobs and Wozniak help develop the Atari game Breakout. The duo also attend meetings of the Homebrew Computer Club. Jobs meets Edwin H. Land, the inventor of instant photography, and models his career after him.

1976—Apple Computer is founded by Steve Jobs (21) and his friend Steve Wozniak (25) on April 1. They begin work out of Jobs's parents' garage.

The Apple I—Apple's first computer—goes on sale in July for $666.66.

1977—The Apple II—Apple's first mainstream computer—goes on sale on April 17. Jobs and Wozniak convince schools across the country to invest in Apple computers.

1980—On December 12, Apple goes public.

1983—The Apple Lisa goes on sale for $9,995 on January 19.

The upgraded Apple II, the Apple IIe, enjoys widespread use in schools.

1984—Apple's "1984" commercial airs for the first time during the Super Bowl in January.

The first Macintosh personal computer goes on sale on January 24. The user can control by pointing and clicking a mouse instead of typing commands.

1985—Jobs and Wozniak are awarded the National Medal of Technology by President Ronald Reagan in February.

Jobs resigns from Apple on September 17.

Jobs starts the company NeXT.

1986—Jobs buys the Graphics Group, which becomes Pixar.

1987—On March 2, the Macintosh II goes on sale.

1991—The PowerBook goes on sale on June 16.

1992—Apple begins the "What's on Your PowerBook" celebrity ad campaign.

1995—Apple introduces the first sitcom-style infomercial, "The Martinettis Bring Home a Computer."

Pixar releases *Toy Story* on November 22.

1996—On December 20, Jobs returns to Apple as an adviser when Apple buys NeXT.

1998—Apple releases the "Think Different" television commercial.

The iMac goes on sale on May 6.

A Bug's Life is released by Pixar on November 25.

1999—On July 2, the iBook goes on sale.

2000—Jobs becomes permanent CEO of Apple.

2001—The iTunes Store opens on January 9.

In May, Apple announces the plan to open 25 retail stores over the year.

The first two Apple retail stores open their doors on May 19.

The iPod is announced on October 23.

On November 10, the iPod goes on sale.

2006—Pixar is sold to Disney.

2007—Jobs unveils the first iPhone on January 9.

On June 27, the iPhone goes on sale.

Apple TV is released.

2009—Jobs announces a leave of absence from Apple due to health reasons in January.

2010—On January 27, Jobs unveils the iPad.

The iPad goes on sale on April 3.

2011—On March 2, Apple announces the iPad2 .

On March 11, the iPad2 goes on sale.

On August 24, Jobs resigns from Apple.

Steve Jobs, Great Inventor

As of October 9, 2011, Jobs was listed as either primary inventor or coinventor of 342 United States patents or patent applications. Most of these are design patents (specific product designs) as opposed to utility patents (inventions). He had 43 issued U.S. patents on inventions. The patent on the Mac OS X dock user interface with magnification feature was issued the day before he died.

You might not know that Jobs is listed, among others, on the patent for the glass staircases seen in larger Apple stores, the little clasp that holds the iPod earbud wires together, or the actual box packaging of the iPhone. It seems that nothing was beyond the reach of his creative mind.

Steve Jobs's Legacy, According to Others

"Steve was among the greatest of American innovators—brave enough to think differently, bold enough to believe he could change the world, and talented enough to do it. By building one of the planet's most successful companies from his garage, he exemplified the spirit of American ingenuity. . . . Steve was fond of saying that he lived every day like it was his last. Because he did, he transformed our lives, redefined entire industries, and achieved one of the rarest feats in human history: he changed the way each of us sees the world." —*President Barack Obama*

"What made Steve Jobs truly great is that he was only interested in doing truly great things." —*U2's Bono*

"Once in a rare while, somebody comes along who doesn't just raise the bar, they create an entirely new standard of measurement." —*Dick Costolo, Twitter CEO*

"Steve and I first met nearly 30 years ago and have been colleagues, competitors and friends over the course of more than half our lives. . . . For those of us lucky enough to get to work with him, it's been an insanely great honor." —*Bill Gates, Microsoft cofounder and chairman*

"His legacy will extend far beyond the products he created or the businesses he built. It will be the millions of people he inspired, the lives he changed, and the culture he defined. . . . Despite all he accomplished, it feels like he was just getting started." —*Bob Iger, Disney CEO*

"The magic of Steve was that while others simply accepted the status quo, he saw the true potential in everything he touched and never compromised on that vision. He leaves behind an incredible family and a legacy that will continue to speak to people for years to come." —*George Lucas*

"We've lost something we won't get back. . . . The way I see it, though, the way people love products he put so much into creating means he brought a lot of life to the world." —*Steve Wozniak, cofounder of Apple Inc.*

When Steve Jobs Spoke, Everyone Listened

"[Bob Dylan is] one of my all-time heroes. . . . His words struck chords of creative thinking."

"What a computer is to me is the most remarkable tool that we have ever come up with. It's the equivalent of a bicycle for our minds."

"[The iTunes music store] will go down in history as a turning point for the music industry. This is landmark stuff. I can't overestimate it!"

"Every once in a while a revolutionary product comes along that changes everything. . . . One is very fortunate if you get to work on just one of these in your career. Apple's been very fortunate it's been able to introduce a few of these into the world."

"My model for business is The Beatles: They were four guys that kept each other's negative tendencies in check; they balanced each other. And the total was greater than the sum of the parts. Great things in business are never done by one person, they are done by a team of people."

"There's an old Wayne Gretzky quote that I love. 'I skate to where the puck is going to be, not where it has been.' And we've always tried to do that at Apple. Since the very very beginning. And we always will."

Bibliography

Beahm, George, ed. *I, Steve: Steve Jobs in His Own Words*. Evanston, IL: Agate B2, 2011.

Cole, Robert J. "An 'Orderly' Debut for Apple" *New York Times*, 13 Dec. 1980.

Editors of Time. *Steve Jobs: The Genius Who Changed Our World*. New York: Time Books, 2011.

Gallo, Carmine. *The Presentation Secrets of Steve Jobs*. New York: McGraw-Hill, 2009.

Isaacson, Walter. *Steve Jobs*. New York: Simon & Schuster, 2011.

Kahney, Leander. *Inside Steve's Brain*. New York: Portfolio, 2009.

Moritz, Michael. *Return to the Little Kingdom: How Apple and Steve Jobs Changed the World*. New York: Overlook Press, 2009.

Pollack, Andrew. "Apple's Lisa Makes a Debut." *New York Times*, 19 Jan. 1983.

Pollack, Andrew. "Apple Computers Entrepreneur's Rise and Fall." *New York Times*, 19 Sept. 1985.

Sandberg-Diment, Erik. "Personal Computers; Hardware Review: Apple Weighs in with Macintosh." *New York Times*, 24 Jan. 1984.

Thomas, Alan Ken, ed. *The Business Wisdom of Steve Jobs*. New York: Skyhorse Publishing, 2011.

Source Notes

(All online sources obtained Nov. 15–17, 2011. Many of the interviews, commercials, product announcements, and videos referenced in *Steve Jobs: American Genius* can be found on *YouTube*.)

Back Cover

"That's been . . ." Reinhardt, Andy. "Steve Jobs: 'There's Sanity Returning.'": *BW Online*. Bloomberg Businessweek, 25 May 1998.

Only Connect

"[Jobs] believed that the computer . . .": Kahney, Leander. "John Sculley on Steve Jobs: The Full Interview Transcript." *Cult of Mac*, 14 Oct. 2010.

"saw the intersection of art and science and business": Bonanos, Christopher. "The Man Who Inspired Jobs." NYTimes.com. *New York Times*, 7 Oct. 2011.

"Technology alone is not enough . . .": Trachtenberg, Stephen Joel, et al. "Career Counselor: Steve Jobs or Bill Gates?" NYTimes.com. *New York Times*, 20 March 2011.

Chapter 1: Origins

"I was born in San Francisco, California . . .": Campanella, Thomas J. "Excerpts from an Oral History Interview with Steve Jobs." Smithsonian Institution Oral and Video Histories. Smithsonian Institution, 20 April 1995.

"a tyrant": "Steve Jobs: An adopted child who never met his biological father." *Telegraph*. Telegraph UK, 6 Oct. 2011.

"upped and left . . .": Dickinson, Georgina. "Dad waits for Jobs to iPhone." *New York Post*, 27 Aug. 2011.

"I think after we . . ." Dickinson, Georgina. "Dad waits for Jobs to iPhone." *New York Post*, 27 Aug. 2011.

"My parents . . .": Isaacson, Walter. *Steve Jobs*. New York: Simon & Schuster, 2011: 5.

"a genius with his hands": Campanella, Thomas J. "Excerpts from an Oral History Interview with Steve Jobs." Smithsonian Institution Oral and Video Histories. Smithsonian Institution, 20 April 1995.

He won the bet . . .: Isaacson, Walter. *Steve Jobs*. New York: Simon & Schuster, 2011: 1.

"He had a workbench . . .": Campanella, Thomas J. "Excerpts from an Oral History Interview with Steve Jobs." Smithsonian Institution Oral and Video Histories. Smithsonian Institution, 20 April 1995.

"Paul was very good . . .": Nijhawan, Avni. "Neighbors Remember Young Steve Jobs." *Los Altos, CA Patch*. Patch Network, 7 Oct. 2011.

"That was my college fund": Lohr, Steve. "Creating Jobs." NYTimes. com. *New York Times*, 12 Jan. 1997.

"the very embodiment . . .": Malone, Michael S. *Infinite Loop*. London: Aurum Press, 1999: 8.

Chapter 2: The Most Wonderful Place to Grow Up

"orchards—apricot orchards . . .": Campanella, Thomas J. "Excerpts from an Oral History Interview with Steve Jobs." Smithsonian Institution Oral and Video Histories. Smithsonian Institution, 20 April 1995.

"That garage would later be dubbed . . .": "The Rise of Silicon Valley." *History of Stanford*. Stanford University, n.d.

"The history of Fairchild . . .": Blank, Steve. "How Silicon Valley Scientists and Engineers Got It Right, and VCs Got It Wrong." *Huff Post Business*. Huffington Post, 25 July 2011.

"It was really the most wonderful place . . .": Campanella, Thomas J. "Excerpts from an Oral History Interview with Steve Jobs." Smithsonian Institution Oral and Video Histories. Smithsonian Institution, 20 April 1995.

"I was always taught . . .": Campanella, Thomas J. "Excerpts from an Oral History Interview with Steve Jobs." Smithsonian Institution Oral and Video Histories. Smithsonian Institution, 20 April 1995.

"These Heathkits would come . . .": Campanella, Thomas J. "Excerpts from an Oral History Interview with Steve Jobs." Smithsonian Institution Oral and Video Histories. Smithsonian Institution, 20 April 1995.

Chapter 3: An Elementary Troublemaker

"School was pretty hard . . .": Campanella, Thomas J. "Excerpts from an Oral History Interview with Steve Jobs." Smithsonian Institution Oral and Video Histories. Smithsonian Institution, 20 April 1995.

"By the time I was in third grade . . .": Campanella, Thomas J. "Excerpts from an Oral History Interview with Steve Jobs." Smithsonian Institution Oral and Video Histories. Smithsonian Institution, 20 April 1995.

"They were going to put Rick . . .": Campanella, Thomas J. "Excerpts from an Oral History Interview with Steve Jobs." Smithsonian Institution Oral and Video Histories. Smithsonian Institution, 20 April 1995.

"She watched me for about two weeks . . .": Campanella, Thomas J. "Excerpts from an Oral History Interview with Steve Jobs."

Smithsonian Institution Oral and Video Histories. Smithsonian Institution, 20 April 1995.

"What was really remarkable . . .": Campanella, Thomas J. "Excerpts from an Oral History Interview with Steve Jobs." Smithsonian Institution Oral and Video Histories. Smithsonian Institution, 20 April 1995.

"My parents said . . .": Campanella, Thomas J. "Excerpts from an Oral History Interview with Steve Jobs." Smithsonian Institution Oral and Video Histories. Smithsonian Institution, 20 April 1995.

"He said he just wouldn't go . . .": Moritz, Michael. *Return to the Little Kingdom: How Apple and Steve Jobs Changed the World*. New York: Overlook Press, 2009: 48.

Chapter 4: A First Job for Jobs

"I saw my first desktop computer . . .": Isaacson, Walter. *Steve Jobs*. New York: Simon & Schuster, 2011: 17.

"Back then, people didn't have . . .": Isaacson, Walter. *Steve Jobs*. New York: Simon & Schuster, 2011: 17.

"Jobs called and asked . . .": "HP Retiree: Quotes and Anecdotes about Bill Hewlett." *Hewlett-Packard*. Hewlett-Packard Development Company, n.d.

"reality distortion . . .": Rao, Arun, and Scaruffi, Piero. "Magicians: Steve Jobs' Reality Distortion Field and Apple Computer (1976–2010)." *A History of Silicon Valley*. Omniware, 1 April 2011.

". . . enthusiastically and grammatically incorrect.": Paltrow, Allen. "My Experience with Jobs and Apple." *Allen Paltrow Tumblr*. Tumblr, 6 Oct. 2011.

Chapter 5: Go-Getter

"You cannot call them collect": Moritz, Michael. *Return to the Little Kingdom: How Apple and Steve Jobs Changed the World*. New York: Overlook Press, 2009: 72.

"I don't have the money . . .": Moritz, Michael. *Return to the Little Kingdom: How Apple and Steve Jobs Changed the World*. New York: Overlook Press, 2009: 72.

"He knew what he was doing": Moritz, Michael. *Return to the Little Kingdom: How Apple and Steve Jobs Changed the World*. New York: Overlook Press, 2009: 74.

Chapter 6: Woz—a Kindred Spirit

"the first person . . .": Isaacson, Walter. *Steve Jobs*. New York: Simon & Schuster, 2011: 25.

"Woz was next door . . .": "Steve Jobs's Childhood Friend Speaks On Icon's Death." *KOAT Albuquerque*. Hearst Properties, Inc., 7 Oct. 2011.

"I never lie . . .": Wozniak, Steve. *iWoz: Computer Geek to Cult Icon: How I Invented the Personal Computer, Co-Founded Apple, and Had Fun Doing It*. New York: W. W. Norton, 2006: 12.

"There were all kinds of interesting things . . .": Wozniak, Steve. *iWoz: Computer Geek to Cult Icon: How I Invented the Personal Computer, Co-Founded Apple, and Had Fun Doing It*. New York: W. W. Norton, 2006: 14.

"When it came down to . . .": Wozniak, Steve. *iWoz: Computer Geek to Cult Icon: How I Invented the Personal Computer, Co-Founded Apple, and Had Fun Doing It*. New York: W. W. Norton, 2006: 18.

"the banner prank that . . .": Isaacson, Walter. *Steve Jobs*. New York: Simon & Schuster, 2011: 26.

"Woz would have it in his pocket . . .": Jobs, Steve. Excerpted from 2007 Macworld Expo keynote address. YouTube, 1 Dec. 2007.

"The makers of Cap'n Crunch . . .": Rosenbaum, Ron. "Secrets of the Little Blue Box." *Secrets of the Little Blue Box.* LosPadres.info, 28 Nov. 1996.

"I felt like . . .": Wozniak, Steve. "History of Hacking." YouTube, 2 May 2008.

"It was, like, four in the morning": Draper, John. "History of Hacking." YouTube, 2 May 2008.

"the first digital . . .": Jobs, Steve. "Silicon Valley: A 100 Year Renaissance." Santa Clara Valley Historical Association. 1 Oct. 1999.

"He's got the whole world . . .": Moritz, Michael. *Return to the Little Kingdom: How Apple and Steve Jobs Changed the World.* New York: Overlook Press, 2009: 85.

Chapter 7: Jobs Tries College

"Steve hung a . . .": Brennan, Chrisann. "The Steve Jobs Nobody Knew." *Rolling Stone,* 12 Oct. 2011.

"degree mill": Moritz, Michael. *Return to the Little Kingdom: How Apple and Steve Jobs Changed the World.* New York: Overlook Press, 2009: 94.

"I naively chose a college . . .": Jobs, Steve. "Stanford Commencement Address." Huffington Post, 5 Oct. 2011.

"We tried to talk him out of it . . .": Moritz, Michael. *Return to the Little Kingdom: How Apple and Steve Jobs Changed the World.* New York: Overlook Press, 2009: 94.

"I didn't even want the buildings . . .": Moritz, Michael. *Return to the*

Little Kingdom: How Apple and Steve Jobs Changed the World. New York: Overlook Press, 2009: 95.

"The minute I dropped out . . .": Jobs, Steve. "Stanford Commencement Address." Huffington Post, 5 Oct. 2011.

"didn't have a dorm room . . .": Jobs, Steve. "Stanford Commencement Address." Huffington Post, 5 Oct. 2011.

"It placed value on experience . . .": Moritz, Michael. *Return to the Little Kingdom: How Apple and Steve Jobs Changed the World.* New York: Overlook Press, 2009: 98.

"returned coke bottles . . .": Jobs, Steve. "Stanford Commencement Address." Huffington Post, 5 Oct. 2011.

"He often didn't want to . . .": Moritz, Michael. *Return to the Little Kingdom: How Apple and Steve Jobs Changed the World.* New York: Overlook Press, 2009: 98.

"Reed College at that time offered . . .": Jobs, Steve. "Stanford Commencement Address." Huffington Post, 5 Oct. 2011.

Chapter 8: Night Shift at Atari

"It was life in the fast lane . . .": Moritz, Michael. *Return to the Little Kingdom: How Apple and Steve Jobs Changed the World.* New York: Overlook Press, 2009: 101.

"It was always chaos . . .": Moritz, Michael. *Return to the Little Kingdom: How Apple and Steve Jobs Changed the World.* New York: Overlook Press, 2009: 103.

"We've got this kid . . .": Alcorn, Al. Ed: "California Extreme: Steve Jobs: From Atari to Apple." *PodTech*, 21 July 2006.

"The engineers didn't like him . . .": Moritz, Michael. *Return to the Little Kingdom: How Apple and Steve Jobs Changed the World.* New York: Overlook Press, 2009: 104.

"I always felt to run a good company . . .": Cifaldi, Frank. "Steve Jobs, Atari Employee Number 40." *Gamasutra*. UBM TechWeb, 7 Oct. 2011.

"Steve I'll cut you a deal . . .": Moritz, Michael. *Return to the Little Kingdom: How Apple and Steve Jobs Changed the World*. New York: Overlook Press, 2009: 104.

"He wasn't dressed appropriately . . .": Alcorn, Al. "California Extreme: Steve Jobs: From Atari to Apple." *PodTech*, 21 July 2006.

Chapter 9: Enlightenment

"the guide to meditation and spirituality . . .": Isaacson, Walter. *Steve Jobs*. New York: Simon & Schuster, 2011: 527.

"We weren't going to find a place . . .": Moritz, Michael. *Return to the Little Kingdom: How Apple and Steve Jobs Changed the World*. New York: Overlook Press, 2009: 106.

Chapter 10: Breakout

"I put him to work again": Alcorn, Al. "California Extreme: Steve Jobs: From Atari to Apple." *PodTech*, 21 July 2006.

"Simple game . . .": Livingston, Jessica. "Steve Wozniak Interview Founders at Work." *Founders at Work*. 26 Jan. 2007.

"We went into Atari every night . . .": Wozniak, Steve. "Steve Wozniak Book Event." YouTube. 3 Oct. 2006.

"My mind was in that state . . .": Wozniak, Steve. "Steve Wozniak Book Event." YouTube. 3 Oct. 2006.

"Nolan Bushnell offered me a job . . .": Livingston, Jessica. "Steve Wozniak Interview—Founders at Work." *Founders at Work*. 26 Jan. 2007.

Chapter 11: Introducing Apple!

"Computer power to the people": Isaacson, Walter. *Steve Jobs*. New York: Simon & Schuster, 2011: 59.

"Are you building your own computer?": Moritz, Michael. *Return to the Little Kingdom: How Apple and Steve Jobs Changed the World*. New York: Overlook Press, 2009: 110.

"This whole vision . . .": Isaacson, Walter. *Steve Jobs*. New York: Simon & Schuster, 2011: 60.

"It was the first microcomputer . . .": Livingston, Jessica. "Steve Wozniak Interview—Founders at Work." *Founders at Work*. 26 Jan. 2007.

"I would design one . . .": Livingston, Jessica. "Steve Wozniak Interview—Founders at Work." *Founders at Work*. 26 Jan. 2007.

"a shortcut computer": Livingston, Jessica. "Steve Wozniak Interview—Founders at Work." *Founders at Work*. 26 Jan. 2007.

"That's really where Steve Jobs came in . . .": Livingston, Jessica. "Steve Wozniak Interview—Founders at Work." *Founders at Work*. 26 Jan. 2007.

"keep in touch": Isaacson, Walter. *Steve Jobs*. New York: Simon & Schuster, 2011: 66.

"I'm keeping in touch": Isaacson, Walter. *Steve Jobs*. New York: Simon & Schuster, 2011: 60.

"I picked [Steve] up . . .": Livingston, Jessica. "Steve Wozniak Interview—Founders at Work." *Founders at Work*. 26 Jan. 2007.

"It was not designed . . .": Livingston, Jessica. "Steve Wozniak Interview—Founders at Work." *Founders at Work*. 26 Jan. 2007.

Chapter 12: Apple Computer, Inc.

"I had color, and then I had graphics . . .": Livingston, Jessica. "Steve Wozniak Interview—Founders at Work." *Founders at Work*. 26 Jan. 2007.

"Every computer now uses switching power . . .": Isaacson, Walter. *Steve Jobs*. New York: Simon & Schuster, 2011: 74.

"I was so smart . . .": Isaacson, Walter. *Steve Jobs*. New York: Simon & Schuster, 2011: 75.

"That was all I needed to know . . .": Livingston, Jessica. "Steve Wozniak Interview—Founders at Work." *Founders at Work*. 26 Jan. 2007.

"We added up to . . .": Livingston, Jessica. "Steve Wozniak Interview—Founders at Work." *Founders at Work*. 26 Jan. 2007.

"Mike really took me under his wing . . .": Isaacson, Walter. *Steve Jobs*. New York: Simon & Schuster, 2011: 78.

"People *DO* judge a book . . .": Isaacson, Walter. *Steve Jobs*. New York: Simon & Schuster, 2011: 78.

Chapter 13: The Rise of Apple, the Fall of Jobs

"I was only twenty-two . . .": Isaacson, Walter. *Steve Jobs*. New York: Simon & Schuster, 2011: 82.

"Woz designed a great machine . . .": Isaacson, Walter. *Steve Jobs*. New York: Simon & Schuster, 2011: 85.

"I remember being at Xerox at 1979 . . .": Campanella, Thomas J. "Excerpts from an Oral History Interview with Steve Jobs." Smithsonian Institution Oral and Video Histories. Smithsonian Institution, 20 April 1995.

"empower . . . people to use the computer . . .": Campanella, Thomas J. "Excerpts from an Oral History Interview with Steve Jobs." Smithsonian Institution Oral and Video Histories. Smithsonian Institution, 20 April 1995.

"Do you want to spend the rest of your life . . .": Rao, Arun, and Scaruffi, Piero. "Magicians: Steve Jobs' Reality Distortion Field and Apple Computer (1976–2010)." *A History of Silicon Valley*. Omniware, 1 April 2011.

"On January 24th, Apple Computer will introduce Macintosh . . .": Apple "1984" television commercial. YouTube. 12 Dec. 2005.

"never trust a computer . . .": CNET News Staff. "Steve Jobs: A timeline." *CNET News*. CNET, 5 Oct 2011.

"The Mac made computing truly personal . . .": Maney, Kevin. "Apple's '1984' Super Bowl commercial still stands as watershed event." USAToday.com. *USA Today*, 28 Jan. 2004.

"global visionary": Rao, Arun, and Scaruffi, Piero. "Magicians: Steve Jobs' Reality Distortion Field and Apple Computer (1976–2010)." *A History of Silicon Valley*. Omniware, 1 April 2011.

"How can you get fired . . .": Jobs, Steve. "Stanford Commencement Address." Huffington Post, 5 Oct. 2011.

"insanely great": Zimmer, Ben. "'And One More Thing': The Insanely Great Language of Steve Jobs." Visual Thesaurus, 7 Oct. 2011.

Chapter 14: Lost and Found

"I didn't see . . .": Jobs, Steve. "Stanford Commencement Address." Huffington Post, 5 Oct. 2011.

"he was never . . .": Simpson, Mona. "A Sister's Eulogy for Steve Jobs." NYTimes.com. *New York Times*, 30 Oct. 2011.

Chapter 15: The NeXT Step

"We basically wanted to keep . . .": Campanella, Thomas J. "Excerpts from an Oral History Interview with Steve Jobs." Smithsonian Institution Oral and Video Histories. Smithsonian Institution, 20 April 1995.

"I was so blown away with the potential . . .": Campanella, Thomas J. "Excerpts from an Oral History Interview with Steve Jobs." Smithsonian Institution Oral and Video Histories. Smithsonian Institution, 20 April 1995.

"object oriented . . .": Campanella, Thomas J. "Excerpts from an Oral History Interview with Steve Jobs." Smithsonian Institution Oral and Video Histories. Smithsonian Institution, 20 April 1995.

"It is now the most popular object . . .": Campanella, Thomas J. "Excerpts from an Oral History Interview with Steve Jobs." Smithsonian Institution Oral and Video Histories. Smithsonian Institution, 20 April 1995.

"The machine was the best machine . . .": Campanella, Thomas J. "Excerpts from an Oral History Interview with Steve Jobs." Smithsonian Institution Oral and Video Histories. Smithsonian Institution, 20 April 1995.

"all software will be written . . .": Campanella, Thomas J. "Excerpts from an Oral History Interview with Steve Jobs." Smithsonian Institution Oral and Video Histories. Smithsonian Institution, 20 April 1995.

"a humiliation akin to . . .": Lohr, Steve. "Creating Jobs." NYTimes.com. *New York Times*, 12 Jan. 1997.

"It was the first time . . .": Lohr, Steve. "Creating Jobs." NYTimes.com. *New York Times*, 12 Jan. 1997.

"a lot of experience . . .": Lohr, Steve. "Creating Jobs." NYTimes. com. *New York Times*, 12 Jan. 1997.

"It's very romantic . . .": Lohr, Steve. "Creating Jobs." NYTimes.com. *New York Times*, 12 Jan. 1997.

Chapter 16: "Sillywood"

"There's a lot of hoopla . . .": Campanella, Thomas J. "Excerpts from an Oral History Interview with Steve Jobs." Smithsonian Institution Oral and Video Histories. Smithsonian Institution, 20 April 1995.

Chapter 17: Think Different

"Apple Computer Inc., after 11 years . . .": Lohr, Steve. "Creating Jobs." NYTimes.com. *New York Times*, 12 Jan. 1997.

"After the first three words . . .": Lohr, Steve. "Creating Jobs." NYTimes.com. *New York Times*, 12 Jan. 1997.

"I trust people more": Lohr, Steve. "Creating Jobs." NYTimes.com. *New York Times*, 12 Jan. 1997.

"I was in the parking lot . . .": Lohr, Steve. "Creating Jobs." NYTimes.com. *New York Times*, 12 Jan. 1997.

"Great products, according to Jobs . . .": Lohr, Steve. "Creating Jobs." NYTimes.com. *New York Times*, 12 Jan. 1997.

"We'd just taken Pixar public . . .": Isaacson, Walter. *Steve Jobs*. New York: Simon & Schuster, 2011: 315.

"If we want Microsoft Office on the Mac . . .": Isaacson, Walter. *Steve Jobs*. New York: Simon & Schuster, 2011: 326.

"For Apple, it's back to the future . . .": Burrows, Peter, and Sager, Ira. "Back to the Future at Apple." *BW Online*. Bloomberg Businessweek, 25 May 1998.

"Act III is under way . . .": Booth, Cathy. "The Comeback Kid." *Time*, August 1997.

Chapter 18: Insanely Great

"shut it down . . .": Markoff, John. "Michael Dell should eat his words, Apple Chief suggests." NYTimes.com. *New York Times*, 16 Jan. 2006.

"Team, it turned out that Michael Dell . . .": Markoff, John. "Michael Dell Should Eat His Words, Apple Chief Suggests." NYTimes.com. *New York Times*, 16 Jan. 2006.

"This is a day . . .": Cohen, Peter. "Macworld Expo Keynote Live Update." Macworld.com. *Macworld*, 9 Jan. 2007.

"The Mac, iPod, Apple TV and . . .": Cohen, Peter. "Macworld Expo Keynote Live Update." Macworld.com. *Macworld*, 9 Jan. 2007.

Chapter 19: Visionary

"there's actually very little distinction between . . .": Campanella, Thomas J. "Excerpts from an Oral History Interview with Steve Jobs." Smithsonian Institution Oral and Video Histories. Smithsonian Institution, 20 April 1995.

"having an insight into what . . .": Campanella, Thomas J. "Excerpts from an Oral History Interview with Steve Jobs." Smithsonian Institution Oral and Video Histories. Smithsonian Institution, 20 April 1995.

"they settle into ways of . . .": Campanella, Thomas J. "Excerpts from an Oral History Interview with Steve Jobs." Smithsonian Institution Oral and Video Histories. Smithsonian Institution, 20 April 1995.

"there will always be opportunity . . .": Campanella, Thomas J. "Excerpts from an Oral History Interview with Steve Jobs."

Smithsonian Institution Oral and Video Histories. Smithsonian Institution, 20 April 1995.

"You've got to have an idea . . .": Campanella, Thomas J. "Excerpts from an Oral History Interview with Steve Jobs." Smithsonian Institution Oral and Video Histories. Smithsonian Institution, 20 April 1995.

"Vic, can you call me . . .": Gundotra, Vic. "Vic Gundotra – Google +." Google +, n.d.

Chapter 20: Live Each Day

"When I was 17 . . .": Jobs, Steve. "Stanford Commencement Address." Huffington Post, 5 Oct. 2011.

"I have always said if there . . .": Jobs, Steve. "Letter from Steve Jobs." Apple.com. Apple Press Info, 24 Aug. 2011.

"Steve was an . . .": Catmull, Ed, and Lasseter, John. Pixar's Statement about Steve Jobs. Pixar.com. Pixar Animation Studios, n.d.

"Apple has lost…": Apple Media Advisory. Apple.com. Apple, Inc., 5 Oct. 2011.

"Steve worked at what he loved . . .": Simpson, Mona. "A Sister's Eulogy for Steve Jobs." NYTimes.com. *New York Times*, 30 Oct. 2011.

Chapter 21: A Dent in the Universe

"We all—in the end . . .": Simpson, Mona. "A Sister's Eulogy for Steve Jobs." NYTimes.com. *New York Times*, 30 Oct. 2011.

"Death is . . .": Jobs, Steve. "Stanford Commencement Address." Huffington Post, 5 Oct. 2011.

"A dent in . . .": Elmer-DeWitt, Philip. "Steve Jobs: Apple's Anti-Gates." Time.com. *Time* magazine, 7 Dec. 1998.

"OH WOW . . .": Simpson, Mona. "A Sister's Eulogy for Steve Jobs." NYTimes.com. *New York Times*, 30 Oct. 2011.

Steve Jobs's Legacy, According to Others

"Steve was among the greatest . . .": Hayes, Mike. "President Obama Responds to the Death of Steve Jobs." Buzzfeed.com. *BuzzFeed*, n.d.

"What made Steve Jobs truly . . .": Fernandez, Sophia M. "Bono on Steve Jobs: We Will All Miss the Hardware Software Elvis." Hollywoodreporter.com. *Hollywood Reporter*, 6 Oct. 2011.

"Once in a rare while . . .": Guynn, Jessica, and Hsu, Tiffany. "Reactions to Steve Jobs' Death." LATimes.com. *Los Angeles Times*, 6 Oct. 2011.

"Steve and I first met nearly . . .": Guynn, Jessica, and Hsu, Tiffany. "Reactions to Steve Jobs' Death." LATimes.com. *Los Angeles Times*, 6 Oct. 2011.

"His legacy will extend far . . .": Moltenbrey, Karen. "Steve Jobs: The industry reflects." Postmagazine.com. *Post*, 6 Oct. 2011.

"The magic of Steve was that . . .": Moltenbrey, Karen. "Steve Jobs: The industry reflects." Postmagazine.com. *Post*, 6 Oct. 2011.

"We've lost something we won't get back . . .": Metz, Rachel. "Steve Wozniak On Steve Jobs' Death." Huffington Post, 6 Oct. 2011.

When Steve Jobs Spoke, Everyone Listened

"[Bob Dylan is] one of my . . .": Greene, Andy. "Steve Jobs Bio Reveals Details of His Relationships With Bob Dylan, Bono." Rollingstone.com. *Rolling Stone*, 24 Oct. 2011.

"What a computer is to me . . .": "Steve Jobs: 20 Best Quotes." Abcnews.com. ABC News, 6 Oct. 2011.

"[The iTunes music store] will . . .": Valentino-DeVries, Jennifer.

"Steve Jobs' Best Quotes." Blogs.wsj.com. *Wall Street Journal*, 24 August 2011.

"Every once in a while . . .": Valentino-DeVries, Jennifer. "Steve Jobs' Best Quotes." Blogs.wsj.com. *Wall Street Journal*, 24 August 2011.

"My model for business is . . .": Ford, Deborah Smith. "Worldwide photo images pay tribute to Steve Jobs." Examiner.com. *Examiner*, 10 Oct. 2011.

"There's an old Wayne Gretzky . . .": "Steve Jobs: 20 Best Quotes." Abcnews.com. ABC News, 6 Oct. 2011.